CANDLE MAN

BOOK TWO

THE SOCIETY
OF DREAD

*Theo crawled on grazed knees as he watched
the stranger's skin bubble and smoke.*

CANDLE MAN

BOOK TWO

THE SOCIETY
OF DREAD

GLENN DAKIN

EGMONT
USA
New York

EGMONT

We bring stories to life

First published by Egmont USA, 2010
443 Park Avenue South, Suite 806
New York, NY 10016

Copyright © Glenn Dakin, 2010
Illustrations copyright © Greg Swearingen, 2009, 2010
All rights reserved

1 3 5 7 9 8 6 4 2

www.egmontusa.com
www.glenndakin.com

Library of Congress Cataloging-in-Publication Data

Dakin, Glenn.
The Society of Dread / Glenn Dakin.
p. cm. — (Candle Man ; bk. 2)
Summary: Now head of the Society of Good Works, teenaged Theo
must reluctantly use his mysterious ability to melt evil when he ventures
underground to face villains of old.
ISBN 978-1-60684-019-1 (hardcover)
[1. Adventure and adventurers—Fiction. 2. Superheroes—Fiction.]
I. Title.
PZ7.D152225Sl 2010
[Fic]—dc22
2010023104

Printed in the United States of America

CPSIA tracking label information:
Random House Production • 1745 Broadway • New York, NY 10019

To Christopher Richard Dakin,
who always said,
"If you don't stand up for yourself,
you don't like yourself."

ONTENTS

CANDLE MAN

BOOK TWO

THE SOCIETY
OF DREAD

CHAPTER 1

A WALK

HOW HARD CAN IT BE?

Theo had never been for a walk before—on his own—but he was pretty sure he could do it. He hunched deeper in his big winter coat, feeling the January chill. The wind ruffled his lank black hair. Cold air sparked tears from his gray eyes. He shivered—he was not used to being outside.

Don't panic, he told himself. *Thousands of people go for walks every day. You can do it.*

He took a deep breath and surveyed the dismal, damp street before him. In the past, he had only been allowed one walk a year—planned by his guardian, Dr. Saint. Now, Dr. Saint was dead. There

1

was no one to tell Theo what to do. In fact, he could do anything he liked.

That was scary.

Theo looked back at the dark shape of Empire Hall, the vast mansion in which he had spent his whole life. Since the death of his guardian, he now owned the great house, even though he was still just a teenager. It was one of the biggest mansions in London, but the sight of it gave Theo no pleasure: it had been little more than a prison to him.

His cautious footsteps had brought him to the Condemned Cemetery, the graveyard that backed onto his house. Dusk was just beginning to gather among its tombs and woodlands. Theo liked dusk. It had always been *his* time, after the dreary routines of the day were over. In his imagination, anything could happen at dusk.

An old man, walking slowly, with a big stick and a plastic earpiece, headed towards him. Theo panicked, thought of turning back—then remembered the words that he needed.

"How do you do?"

The old man frowned at Theo, grunted, and moved on.

Theo's heart was pounding, but he was happier

now. He had faced a tricky encounter, but his book
An Introduction to Introductions had saved him.

*When meeting a stranger or new acquaintance, the
traditional formula of "How do you do" is all that is
required*, the book stated.

The wrought-iron gates of the cemetery were
open, a thin mist covering the ground within like
a gray sea. He stepped inside, all senses alert. His
long coat dragged through the dank nettles and
outlandish weeds of the overgrown place.

Theo peered around. He eyed the stone figures
and angels with fascination. He knew from experience that such things could come to life. But nothing
like that happened now. In fact, on this drippy, slow,
January afternoon, the world seemed quiet and
empty of excitement. Dead.

That was just how Theo liked it.

Turning back, he could see the lights were being
switched on in Empire Hall. It was hard to believe
that the daily routine of the household was going on
without his presence.

A strange sensation stirred him from within, like
a breeze whispering in his heart. A feeling grew that
he barely recognized or understood: freedom.

It was wonderful to know that now his evil guardian was dead he could start living a normal life —for

the first time. How delicious it was to breathe the soft, damp air and smell the curious scents of the overgrown cemetery. He walked through the rows of tombs, gazing at every weathered stone carving, solemn inscription, and tattered bouquet. For someone who had never been taken to a beauty spot, a park, or a garden, this graveyard was a world of wonders.

Just a bit longer, he told himself as he ducked under the ragged hawthorn trees and ventured deeper into the cemetery. Theo saw a narrow, almost invisible pathway between holly trees and followed it, taking delight in the sparkling cobwebs among the drippy thorns, the bright red berries, the brown and golden ferns curling in the chill air.

This is a magical place, Theo thought. *I wish I could wander here forever.*

Suddenly he glanced down at his hands—at the leather gauntlets he wore at all waking hours. A pale, green light was flickering about his fingers. He frowned. His power was stirring. That was a sure sign of danger . . . but why now?

"At last!"

Theo's thoughts were shattered by a booming voice. A giant figure broke through the holly trees and loomed over him.

A pale man with a shaven head and strange bulbous eyes confronted him. He was dressed in a filthy, ill-fitting collection of rags. His immense, powerful hands were dark with ingrained dirt. As he approached, Theo he lifted his broad, ugly nose in a sniffing gesture, like a wary animal.

"You don't know who—or what—I am, do you?" the figure snarled.

Theo held his breath but he tried not to panic. He didn't need to know who this was. He just had to find the words to say.

"How do you do?" he blurted out quickly.

The man lashed out with a big leather boot and kicked Theo's legs from under him. Theo crashed to the ground, almost fainting from pain and shock.

"How do I do?" growled the man. "How do I do, when you and your friends wrecked all our plans and destroyed our home?"

"I—we—what?" gasped Theo, astonished.

His mind raced. He *had* seen men like this before. Among the armies of Dr. Saint, there had been many shaven-headed, powerful brutes: Foundlings, they were called. But this one seemed somehow different—almost like a wild man. Theo's hands were deep in nettles, and, unseen by the attacker, he began to work off his gloves.

5

"Don't act all innocent," the man cried. "You've had your fun, but it's all over now!" He paused, his protruding eyes glinting, as if savoring Theo's plight. "*He's* back," the man said with a nasty smile. "And he's more powerful than Dr. Saint ever was. He's back and now you're finished!"

He's back? Who was *he*? Theo wondered as he tried to edge away.

"They told me you were special—you had some kind of magic," the menacing figure said. "Well, I've never believed in magic, and I don't think you'll have much left when I've pulled your heart, lungs, an' liver out."

He moved in on Theo, who was desperately scrambling backwards through the weeds. Theo had taken his gloves off and nettles were stinging his skin.

"I've bided my time," the man said. "I've come to the surface, kept a watch, and waited for a chance to pay you back."

He wrenched Theo up from the ground and swung him backwards, about to dash his head against a gravestone.

But he never did. Theo's trailing hand made contact—the barest whisper of a touch—with the man's cheek. The attacker could not move. He stared

6

down at his own body as it began to glow a luminous green.

Theo fell to the ground. He crawled on grazed knees as he watched the stranger's skin bubble and smoke. Then, the angry, frightened face of the man smeared downwards, a gaping skull shining out from the ruins of the flesh.

With a whooshing *hiss*, the man melted into a big steaming pool.

"Theo!"

Theo had climbed onto a stone tomb, to avoid being touched by the hot slime. Through the bushes came a familiar figure in a navy greatcoat and peaked cap.

It was Chloe. She took in the scene with a glance, clapping her hands to her head in dismay.

"Theo, you idiot!"

◆◆◆

The dark bookshelves towered above them on both sides, as Theo and Chloe sat together on an old leather sofa, deep in the library of Empire Hall.

"He was a Sewer Rat," Chloe said, still huddled in her enormous coat although they were back indoors. "That is, if I can rely on your colorful description of the fiend." There was a twinkle in her eyes as she said this. They both knew that Theo was remarkably observant. "Part of a gang that lives beneath London—in the network of tunnels you love so much."

"A Sewer Rat?"

Chloe put on her official face. As a member of the secret group that protected Theo, the Society of Unrelenting Vigilance, she held arcane knowledge that never failed to astonish him.

"Your evil guardian, Dr. Saint, sometimes used criminal gangs to do his dirty work for him. The Sewer Rats are a loose association of ne'er-do-wells that live in the tunnels and sewers beneath this city. Scuzzbags. You could call them urban pirates."

"Pirates?" Theo's eyes suddenly lit up. "Well, he did look a bit like one. But he did this funny sniffing thing," Theo said, aping the Sewer Rat's upturned nose and his big staring eyes.

"Thanks for sharing," commented Chloe dryly. "Some of them have gone feral down there, half wild, and really do live like rats. They hate the surface world now. They take these funny potions so they can see better in the dark. Makes their eyes stick out. It's horrible."

"But why did he hate me?" Theo asked.

Chloe looked thoughtful. "It's not hard to guess.

When you defeated Dr. Saint, you ruined the hopes of all the assorted scum that worked for him, including the dregs like the Sewer Rats. They'll probably never forgive you for defeating their paymaster."

Theo looked gloomy. Being a hero was more complicated than he realized. Everything you did seemed to lead to more trouble.

"Looks like one of these thugs tried to make a name for himself by getting revenge on you," Chloe concluded.

"I didn't want to melt him," Theo said. "I—I had no choice."

"I didn't call you an idiot for defending yourself." Chloe sighed. "I just can't believe you went out on your own." Her brow knitted into the fine lines Theo knew so well. "Especially without telling me!"

Theo peered through the back window that opened onto a little courtyard. It was now dark outside. His breath made a cloud of mist on the pane. He dabbed his finger in it, childishly, and drew a glum face.

"I thought it would be all right. I thought all the trouble was over now."

Chloe frowned.

"Don't be dense, Theo!" she whispered. "Look, like it or not, you are the Candle Man, the latest incarnation of an ancient hero. Sadly, that means you inherit a lot of enemies too."

Theo looked bleak. He didn't like hearing about his terrifying destiny.

"But, looking on the bright side," Chloe continued, "you also inherit an ancient society whose job it is to look after you: the Society of Unrelenting Vigilance. This crazy group of fanatics is one I'm rather proud to be a member of." She gave a weary smile. "You might at least help me a bit by telling me when you're taking a stroll with a bug-eyed assassin!"

Theo responded with a wary grin. "And you also have a duty to protect me," he said, "because you're in the police."

"Yes, our old leader, Mr. Norrowmore, thought that would make me especially useful to the cause," Chloe remarked. "I suppose where you're concerned I'm a kind of double agent," she added.

"And so I'm double protected," Theo replied, feeling brighter. Now that Chloe was there to talk to, he was already starting to forget the shock of the attack.

"But we have to face facts. There are sinister people out there who don't want a new Candle Man stalking the streets! Dr. Saint may be dead, but he had allies, armies of villains at his command. I tried to make a list of your possible enemies last night, and guess what—I ran out of paper."

"Ha-ha—good one," groaned Theo.

"I'm not joking!" Chloe said. She looked thoughtful. "He is back," she said, musing on the words of the attacker. "That's what's bothering me. If only we knew who 'he' was . . ."

Suddenly she jumped up.

"Wait!" she mouthed at Theo. She put a finger to her lips and, in a swift movement, darted to the library door.

Theo watched. The doorknob was slowly turning. He crept to Chloe's side. They held their breaths as the door began to creak open.

"Down!" Chloe nudged Theo, urging him to take shelter behind a bookcase.

A lumbering, dark form appeared in the doorway, along with a clinking and rattling sound.

"Hot cocoa, sir?" boomed a deep, musical voice.

The butler, Montmerency, entered with a tea trolley. Chloe laughed and flopped back down in her chair.

"Bring it on," she said eagerly.

"You see," Theo said with a smile as the butler departed, "things aren't always as scary as they look."

"Well, things are pretty bad," Chloe insisted, helping herself to some chocolate biscuits. "But there's one thing we do have on our side: you."

Chloe wiggled her fingers in imitation of Theo using his powers. Theo sighed. He didn't like it when she did that. He sat back and sipped his cocoa.

"We've also got you," he said. "So I'm sure we'll win in the end. Don't worry, Chloe. Dr. Saint is beaten. I escaped from the Sewer Rat. The bad old days will soon be over."

Chloe frowned into her steaming mug.

"The bad old days are never over," she said.

CHAPTER 2

TRICKY

THE CORRIDOR OF DOOM lay before Theo. Well, Chloe called it that, anyway. The Boardroom was at the end of a long, windowless passage of shiny marble. Some parts of Empire Hall, long forbidden to him by his guardian, still scared him.

"You don't have to go through with this, Theo," she said. "You're still not a hundred percent—according to the doctors. And you had a nasty shock yesterday."

"I'll be all right," Theo said.

It was mid-afternoon, and, in the best suit that Montmerency could dig out for him at short notice, Theo prepared to meet the charity he was now supposed to be head of.

"The Society of Good Works," said Chloe, peeking through the half-opened door into the shadowy boardroom, "was invented by a Victorian gentleman, as a cover for the wickedest criminal organization in the world."

She tried to straighten Theo's tie, then gave up.

"Some people aren't meant to look well groomed," she observed. "When it comes to personal style, I think you do 'weird' a lot better."

"I want to have this meeting," Theo said. "I need to talk to them. I need everyone to know that things have changed."

"Things have certainly changed," said Chloe. "Dr. Saint and his villainous cronies are all dead, under arrest, or on the run. Today you're addressing their next of kin, legal heirs, and representatives. No one in this room is under official police suspicion—but don't trust them. Even Dr. Saint had trouble controlling Board Meetings. They'll be tricky."

Theo stepped nervously through the door. The curtains were drawn and the room was dark inside. Montmerency had suggested holding the meeting in this way, according to the ancient traditions of the Society; the shadows suited the generally secretive nature of its activities. Theo wished he had changed that tradition now.

14

He stood at the head of the table, and Chloe sat in the corner by the door. Dark silhouettes met his gaze at every side. Silence, so thick you could almost touch it, hovered in the musty air.

Theo stood, gaping.

"Go on," Chloe whispered.

"Err . . . Society of Good Works," Theo began, his voice sounding funny to his own ears in that vast room. "Dr. Saint is dead, and I, Theo Wickland, through no choice of my own, am the new head of this Society."

Theo stopped. Silence. In the darkness he could feel eyes upon him. For a moment he felt like running away. He glanced at Chloe and saw her stifling a yawn. Somehow, this made him feel better. He had prepared a speech and was determined to deliver it.

Except Theo was not used to people actually listening to him. After spending much of his childhood as a virtual prisoner, he wasn't used to people, full stop. He took a deep breath.

"Years ago," he said, "someone had a great idea for a charity: the Society of Good Works."

Silence.

"But then, it went wrong," Theo continued. "It became a wicked, evil, criminal gang."

15

None of the Board seemed to react. Theo gulped.

"That is all over now," he said. "The old leaders of this Society have been arrested. Now is the time to make a new start. From now on, this will be a real Society of Good Works, performing"—he struggled for words for a moment—"err . . . real good works!" he concluded.

Another moment of silence. The dark figures around the table stirred. Suddenly a loud noise made Theo jump.

It was applause. To Theo's relief, the table erupted in a huge round of cheers and clapping. He fell back in his chair, astonished and relieved.

"I say, can someone put the light on?" came a voice from the back. "I can't see a blasted thing."

"Good idea," said Chloe. "I'm falling asleep here."

Someone found a light switch. Theo blinked as lamps began to shine in every corner of the room. Theo was surprised to see that the sinister figures were, in fact, nearly all as young as he.

At the far end of the table, a smartly dressed young man, in a sleek black frock coat, was slouched in a big leather chair. It was he who had called for the lights to come on.

"Freddie Dove," said the young man, rising. "May I just say, on behalf of the rest of the Board, that we are with you all the way! A *real* society of good works! At last! Just what we need!"

For this, Freddie received another round of applause.

"And may I add, that if my wicked father, Lord Dove, was here," he continued in a cool, confident voice, "I would gladly run him through with my rapier!"

Freddie acted out this imaginary piece of swordsmanship for the benefit of the room, to slightly more muted applause.

"I don't care who your parents are—or what they did," Theo added, smiling. "I want this to be a new age—a new start for everyone."

Somebody started singing "For He's a Jolly Good Fellow," and then the whole room joined in—except Chloe.

"One item of business," piped up Freddie again. "When will our network of underground tunnels be open again?"

"I realize that everyone here wants life to return to normal. The network has been damaged since the great battle," Theo said. "But a team is being sent down straightaway to investigate any damage and make repairs."

Someone started singing "For He's a Jolly Good Fellow" again.

Theo wasn't sure how to react. But when he began to join in the chorus, Chloe gave him a swift kick on the ankle.

Theo left the room to a standing ovation.

"See? I told you things weren't as bad as they look," he said to Chloe outside. "They like me. No one wants the bad old days back. They just want the network open again and a chance to make amends."

Chloe frowned. "I told you they would be tricky!"

CHAPTER 3

NEW AGE

ELL, ARE YOU READY for the new age of friendship and cooperation?" Chloe asked with a slight smile as she helped Sam load a bundle of tools into a gigantic iron wheelbarrow. Late, low sun sparkled in the icy puddles of the old graveyard. Even the dead heads of decayed weeds were golden in its rays.

Theo was pleased to see his friends all gathered together outside the cemetery keeper's cottage. There was Magnus, the graveyard keeper; Sam the grave digger, his grandson; and, of course, Chloe. It wasn't often the whole Society of Unrelenting Vigilance were united in one place.

"This is an important time in the great history of our Society," Magnus croaked. He was bundled up in a shapeless army-surplus trench coat and a mustard-colored scarf. The old man paused for breath, leaning on a pair of battered walking sticks. "A chance to sweep away the grudges of old."

Chloe frowned. "Blah, blah," she remarked lightly. "But are you sure this expedition is a good idea?"

"You saw them," said Theo. "You were there. The new generation of the Society of Good Works just wants to be friends. All they ask is that the network is up and running again, so they can use it as they have done for a hundred years."

Chloe scowled. "Use it for smuggling, spying, and skulking."

Magnus flicked an enormous rubber-covered flashlight on and off to check that it was working.

"They are a proud, if misguided, Society—a band of ancient, once noble families ruined by wealth and privilege. Like us, they are a relic of another age. None of us fit into this new world of computers and rocket ships."

Sam snorted. "Computers aren't new," he groaned. "And neither are rocket ships. Even you must know that, Grandad."

Magnus ignored him. "The point is, I can feel pity

for my enemies," he said. "They lost friends, hopes, a whole way of life when Dr. Saint was defeated. He convinced them the Society of Good Works was destined to rule this city. They thought he was a great visionary. No one realized until too late that he was falling under the power of dark alchemy. He led them on a reckless path that ended in ruin. But now we have a chance to show them kindness and end the old wars."

"And who better to help them repair the network than us?" Sam grinned. "We've got the ancient map that Theo discovered. It reveals lost tunnels that have been forgotten for years."

Theo knew he could rely on Sam for a bit of enthusiasm. The young gravedigger had a surprisingly cheery nature—considering his occupation. As Sam continued to load up the barrow with equipment, his fair hair gleamed in the late sun and his generally ruddy face was bright red from his exertions.

"I wish I was going down too," Theo said.

"Well, I don't," Chloe retorted. "After that incident with the Sewer Rat, I want you where I can keep an eye on you."

"I'd feel a lot better going down there with the Candle Man by my side," said Sam.

Chloe sighed. "You know what Theo's like, Sam," she said with a grin. "He's a danger magnet. Take Theo with you and you'll probably be followed by a horde of smoglodytes or end up at a garghoul's wedding."

Sam guffawed, but Theo felt a little dismayed. Sometimes Chloe's jokes struck uncomfortable chords of truth.

"Anyway," said Sam, "if there was any trouble, Theo would sort it out like he did that man who attacked him. *Zap! Splosh!*"

Theo turned away from the others. He was supposed to be a hero, but the idea of his power still churned his stomach and filled him with revulsion.

Sam shoved the wheelbarrow of equipment over the rutted ground as they headed off. Magnus fumbled in his fingerless woolen gloves to triple-lock the cottage door.

"Theo," the cemetery keeper said in a low tone, encouraging Theo to lag behind the others as they trudged towards Kensington Gore. "Beware! I feel something. The invisible, approaching footprint of an enemy."

"An enemy?"

"Don't forget the words of that Sewer Rat," Magnus said. " 'He' is back. Beware whoever 'He' is."

Theo looked miserable. "I—I've only been the Candle Man for a couple of months," he said. "I've told everyone that I just want to make friends and forget the past. How can I already have enemies?"

Magnus stopped and glowered down at Theo with a look that was almost frightening.

"Because light," he said, "doth cast shadows!"

Theo gulped.

"There is one more thing," Magnus said. "A further portent." They were in sight of the street now, where a large gray van was waiting for them. The old man stopped under a great, bare, ruined old oak.

"Yes?"

"All is not well in the cemetery," Magnus said. "There is a disturbance in the yard." Magnus gestured at the great field of sloping graves and tumbledown mausoleums. The door of the nearest tomb hung slightly ajar, as if inviting morbid curiosity.

"Bones have gone missing," Magnus said in a low tone. "Robbed out of old tombs. Graves have been found open, with no remains to be found inside."

"Is—is that normal?" Theo asked feebly.

Magnus's shriveled lips puckered in a small smile. "Theo, this is a graveyard, not a library," he said darkly. "We don't lend bones out."

"Room for one more?" a haughty voice called out as the Network Repair Team clambered into the big unmarked gray van outside Empire Hall. Sam and Magnus had boarded first, followed by a crew of engineers and security guards.

The van was ready to set off for the Monarch Fields pumping station—the Society of Good Works' traditional point of entry to the network.

Theo, who was ready to wave Sam and Magnus off, was surprised to see a figure he recognized, in a stylish frock coat, appear by the driver's window.

"Let me in the front with you, driver," he said. "I'm not getting in the back with all the riffraff!"

It was Freddie Dove.

"I'm sorry, sir," the driver said. "You're not on the mission list."

"I am now," said Freddie, walking round to let himself into the front passenger seat.

He gave Theo a little half-bow before getting in.

"Got to keep an eye on my interests, Theo. I hear there's a world of wonders down there." He flashed a smile as he slammed the door.

Theo watched the van drive off into the London twilight.

"That's what I like to see," he said. "A bit of enthusiasm."

"Charming fellow," said Chloe. "Wonder if he's brought his rapier?"

CHAPTER 4

UNMASKED

"IT'S FOR YOU, SIR," Montmerency the butler said, calling Theo over to the telephone in the main hallway. Theo had just finished a late supper of millet broth and had been pondering whether to go up to bed.

Maybe it will be Sam calling from the network entrance at Monarch Fields, Theo thought. *I wonder if they managed to get down the main shaft there yet.*

He picked up the antique instrument, taking great care to get the mouth and earpiece the right way round.

"I need to see you," Chloe said urgently. "Can you meet me at the gates of the cemetery, right about now?"

Theo nodded.

"I can't hear you—are you there?" Chloe asked suddenly.

"Of course I'm here—I just nodded, didn't I?" Theo said. He heard an exasperated noise at the other end of the line.

"Theo, it's a phone," Chloe groaned. "I can't see you nod your head! Are you trying to win idiot of the week?"

"I'm not used to them yet," Theo said. "Dr. Saint never let me use one." He tugged at the tangled wire. The main landline at Empire Hall was inconveniently located next to an immense, potted aspidistra plant.

"And I've got a plant in my face," he added.

"Well, I've got the whole of Scotland Yard in my face," said Chloe, "and half of the Home Office. You've turned into an issue. Finley says he's discovered something and he needs a meeting tonight. He's in the Condemned Cemetery right now."

Moments later, hastily wrapped in his long black coat, with a woolly hat pulled down over his ears, Theo met Chloe at the gates of the Condemned Cemetery. The night was freezing, and Theo could see his steamy breath plume out under the gateway lamps. Chloe was wearing her enormous navy greatcoat, with her familiar peaked cap angled low over her eyes.

"I was dragged into headquarters today," Chloe said. "Some new bloke called Gold is in charge. Suddenly everyone at Scotland Yard is on their toes. You will not believe the hassle I'm going through. And guess what it's all about? You! That's why I asked you to meet me here."

"You know it's past my bedtime," Theo said.

"Ever the great adventurer," Chloe remarked.

She led Theo through the dark headstones at a pace he found rather tiring. His guardian had never allowed him much exercise, and now any kind of physical activity took its toll quickly.

They brushed through the little holly wood that bordered the cemetery keeper's cottage. In front of the house stood the policemen they knew well—Inspector Finley and Sergeant Crane. Finley was impressive as ever in his vast beige coat, a Russian fur hat, and a neatly tucked-in gray scarf. Crane cut an almost comical figure in shiny black shoes and the ghastly suede jacket he was so fond of.

As he approached the policemen, Theo noticed they were studying him with keen interest. Finley loomed over him, ominously silent, and Theo waited anxiously, a strange sinking feeling in his stomach.

"We know who you are," Finley said at last.

Theo blinked. He gulped. He opened his mouth but no words would come out.

"Yes," Finley continued. "We've finally worked it out. Despite the attempts by Special Detective Cripps to hide your identity under a smokescreen of confusing and misfiled reports."

"Or," added Crane wryly, "by using something we in the police call 'lies.'"

Theo looked at Chloe. The game was up.

"You're Candle Man," Finley stated.

For an instant, it seemed to Theo as if every frosty tree in the graveyard was suddenly listening to their conversation.

"Some of the villains from the Society of Good Works who we arrested recently have been blabbing. Your name kept coming up," Finley explained.

"You can melt people," blurted out Sergeant Crane with a strange relish.

Theo had gone white.

"Are . . . Are you going to put me in prison?" he asked.

For a moment there was a surprised silence. Then, to his astonishment, Sergeant Crane laughed.

This was followed by a kind smile from Finley.

"Certainly not," Finley said.

"You're a hero!" Crane blurted out.

"We've been reading the old Wickland file in Scotland Yard's Black Museum," Finley continued. "We know that the original Candle Man worked closely with the law—especially with a certain Inspector Edward Rooke. Dark days. Most of the files don't make pretty reading."

Theo's eyes lit up.

"You've got files—real stories about the Candle Man?" he gasped. "Can I read them?"

"Told you," muttered Chloe, looking away.

"Maybe," replied the inspector. "But we need to get one thing clear. Like your ancestor, you must use your power in cooperation with the police."

Theo looked away from the inspector, down at his feet.

"I—don't want to," he said quietly.

"Don't want to?"

Theo looked up, his eyes clear, his voice calm and decided.

"I've told everyone," he said. "I don't want to go around melting people and making enemies. I just want to help people—if I can."

Inspector Finley looked grave. "The original

Candle Man helped Scotland Yard," he said, "during an evil time for this city. Now, I'm afraid to say, those dark days are returning."

"Hold on a minute," Chloe said, hopping from one foot to the other, trying to keep warm. "Why are we having this conversation in a freezing graveyard at midnight—when we could be arguing in your cozy office?"

Finley looked grave.

"Ah," he said. "That's just it. You see, we might have a spot of Candle-Manning for our young friend here," he said. He turned to the other officer. "Sergeant Crane, how are our teams doing?" he asked.

Crane exchanged swift radio messages with the police teams that were stationed elsewhere throughout the cemetery.

"This way," he said.

Theo was uneasy. What did the police have in mind? Suddenly all the efforts of his day caught up with him and he felt almost faint. Chloe seemed to sense this and grabbed him by the arm.

"I wasn't expecting this, Theo," she said. "If you don't like it, just say so. I'll stand up for you."

"We ... We'd better see what the inspector wants," said Theo.

"We've got a signal!" hissed Crane. "Come on!"

Now everyone was running along a narrow track. Flashlight beams danced in the darkness. Crane shone his light on a great stone casket, with a headless angel standing at one end.

"Stop here," Crane ordered. They stood in a little grove about a hundred yards from the tomb. Theo could see a police officer pointing a scanning device, not unlike a metal detector, towards the foot of the grave.

"Ground-penetrating radar," explained Crane with a nod.

"What's going on?" Theo asked anxiously. He could feel the trap closing around him, his grim fate taking over from the quiet life he sought.

"*Bones*," said Sergeant Crane. "Bones disappearing from graveyards all over London."

"With no sign of the graves being touched . . . *above* ground," added Inspector Finley.

Crane nodded. "Plenty of evidence of them being taken . . . from below!" he concluded, almost smugly.

"Below?" Theo couldn't help but sound intrigued.

"Coming in now," the radar man whispered.

As they all watched, spellbound, the headless angel on top of the tomb started to tremble.

"This is it!" said Crane, peering over the shoulder of the radar operative. "This is the contact we've been waiting for!"

The stone angel suddenly toppled to the ground. The walls of the tomb shuddered.

"Go, go, go!" roared Finley.

Sergeant Crane raced to the tomb, pulling out his gun. Theo looked on, astonished, as Crane shone his flashlight down into the shattered grave.

"There's an eye! An eye down there!" he cried out in horror. In the darkness, Theo saw something that looked like a dark root grip Crane's ankle. Crane yelled as he was dragged to the ground.

Suddenly the soil erupted. Chunks of rock flew outwards, cutting into Theo's shins and bringing him gasping to his knees. Finley covered his eyes as grit hit his face.

Theo staggered up and stumbled forwards. It was hard to make out what was happening in the darkness.

"No!" came a pitiful cry. Crane was hanging on to the cracked edge of the tomb for dear life, trying not to be pulled into the darkness.

"Theo! Do something!" Chloe shouted.

Theo tore off his gloves; already his fingers were aglow. He grabbed the long feeler that was dragging

Crane downwards. It seemed to freeze for a moment, then glowed bright green. An unearthly scream rent the air as the feeler lit up, writhing and crackling, smoke streaming from it.

"I—I'm free!" shouted Crane. Finley began to pull up his comrade. Suddenly more feelers appeared, bursting from the ground and coiling everywhere, like dark snakes. Theo heard a gasp from Chloe.

By the light of his own hands, he saw her being engulfed in black tendrils. Theo reached out, his hands on fire, but a dark root snared his leg and sent him sprawling to the ground.

"Chloe!" cried Sergeant Crane, brandishing his gun.

"Don't shoot!" roared Finley. "You might hit her!"

"Theo!" Chloe screamed as her body was dragged into the yawning darkness of the tomb.

Suddenly the ground beneath them trembled. There was a dull rumble. The walls of the tomb caved inwards, the gaping hole snapped shut.

Chloe was gone.

CHAPTER 5

UNLUCKY

"IT'S NO GOOD," said Sergeant Crane. "We've lost her!"

It was past midnight in the Condemned Cemetery. A large crowd of policemen had gathered around the collapsed tomb into which Chloe had vanished.

Theo stared helplessly at the ground. He sank to his knees and clawed his hands into the icy dirt. His fingers flickered with impotent green fire. The earth would not respond to his power.

"What . . . What are we up against?" muttered Finley, aghast. "What would that thing want with her?"

"See?" said Sergeant Crane. "See now why we need a Candle Man?"

All eyes looked to Theo, but he stalked off, distractedly, into the woods, his eyes scouring the tree roots and hollows as if seeking some other opening — some way to follow Chloe.

"There's no way through," one of the technicians said, pointing his radar scanner at the tomb. "The ground is solid again. Whatever took her has the power to tunnel effortlessly beneath us, then cover all its traces."

In the nearby woods, Theo stopped suddenly.

A dark shadow blocked his way.

"There's no other way, Theo!" Finley was saying, back at the broken tomb. "This city needs its Candle Man — as it did long ago."

There was a murmur among the officers gathered.

"I would be down there too, Theo — if it wasn't for you," added Sergeant Crane, nursing a cut hand.

"Theo?"

The policemen turned from the tomb and gazed around them. Their torch beams flickered here and there but found only silent trees, slanted gravestones, and weathered statues.

Theo had vanished.

Theo could feel his bones rattling with cold, his eyes streaming with tears as he clung on to the stony body of the winged creature that lifted him through the air. It was Tristus the garghoul, his friend.

Over the holly wood, above the ancient yew forest, and beyond the silent mausoleums they passed.

"Here," Tristus said, setting Theo down just outside the back gate of the cemetery. "We may still be in time."

Theo immediately recognized the place where they had landed. Before them, a circular iron hatch, surrounded by frosted weeds, glittered in the starlight. To most people it appeared to be an old sewer maintenance cover. But to Theo it was a way into the place he both loved and dreaded—the network.

"Chloe—" Theo began to speak as the garghoul rapped on the hatch's central plaque, *tip-tap-tip*, commanding it to open.

There was a hiss of air, and the pale glow of yellow light from the fungus globes within.

"Your friend was taken—I know," the garghoul replied, darting into the tunnel and looking sharply this way and that. "They may not have gone far!"

Just hearing the garghoul's clear, beautiful voice

seemed to fill Theo's heart with hope and his limbs with renewed energy.

The garghoul led the way, taking Theo into passages he had never trodden before. The mazy ways of the old tunnels were bewildering, but Theo could tell he was being led back under the cemetery.

They soon emerged into an underground chamber lit by a single fungus globe. The dim lamp was one of many located throughout the network, glass balls of bioluminescent plant matter. This one hung awkwardly from a drooping bracket and revealed shattered walls, crazed with great cracks.

"There!" Theo shrieked.

The tail end of a black tendril slipped over the edge of a shaft by the far wall. In a flash, the garghoul swooped in pursuit, disappearing after its quarry in a flurry of batlike wings.

Theo waited in the chamber, his heart pounding.

It's back, he said to himself. *The world of the Candle Man is back.*

He could hardly believe that in such a short time he had been taken from his cozy room in Empire Hall and plunged back into this world of peril.

Chloe. Tristus has to rescue Chloe.

Theo started, sensing a movement behind him.

He looked around but saw nothing—only his own shadow against the wall, distorted by the fungus globe.

Where am I? Theo wondered. After surviving his first adventure in the network two months ago, he had studied the map of the underground realm every night. Yet the tunnels still yielded endless surprises. Something on the map that appeared to be a mere slip of the pen could turn out to be a place of lost significance, a splendid ruin, or a pitted death trap.

This must have been an important junction once, Theo reflected. He knew that the original Candle Man, Lord Wickland, had fought many battles, solved many mysteries in this great labyrinth beneath London. As he stood there he could almost imagine the ghost of his great ancestor walking by at any second, his hands aglow, his bright eyes kindled with great purpose, forever stalking mysterious foes.

Theo stood, trembling with cold and anxiety, as his mind sought to contemplate everything—except the loss of his dearest friend.

No!

The garghoul sprang out of the shaft—alone.

"It escaped me," Tristus said. The horned creature looked grim. "Truly you do have the eyes of the

Candle Man, to have spotted that creature before a garghoul did."

Theo joined Tristus on the brink of the shaft. "What was it?"

"Something I have never seen before," Tristus replied. "A mystery," he added in a tone of astonishment. "I thought I had grown too old for them."

"How—?" Theo's voice cracked with emotion. "How did it get away?"

Tristus's brow darkened. "There are cracks and shafts like this running through the entire network now," he said. "The whole place was damaged by the great explosion that ended your battle with Dr. Saint. This thing—these foul creatures—must be using the cracks to come to the surface unseen. Once lost in the shadows they could disappear in countless ways."

"But what about Chloe?" Theo asked. "Why would they take her?"

Tristus's eyes seemed to turn ice-cold, like white fire.

"I do not know," he replied simply.

"But you—" Theo began in a pained voice. "You seem to know everything."

Tristus looked away from Theo, as if unable to bear the boy's gaze.

"I have been watching over the graveyard," Tristus said. "It is the way of garghouls to watch — and wait. I was aware that these vile things were on the move — but until now I was happy to consider it none of my business."

"Then what is your business?"

Tristus looked grim. "You are. When you appeared in the cemetery tonight, of course I kept my eye on you — but I was too late to prevent the taking of your friend."

"What can we do?"

"'We' can't do anything," Tristus said. "I can seek for these creatures best on my own."

"You could carry me."

"I have done so before. But I carried you *from* peril — not into it. I will not be responsible for taking a soft, breakable mortal into the depths of this deadly labyrinth. Even one who possesses the rare tripudon energy, as you do. I suggest you return home as swiftly as you can and gather your strength. But for now, every second you argue could endanger your friend."

Theo glanced back the way he had come. He nodded. He would know the way back. But abandoning the pursuit now was bitter.

"You once told me," Theo said, "that I would be

very unlucky if I ever needed your friendship again."

Tristus rose on his beating wings and poised above the shaft.

"We have been unlucky," he said.

Theo watched the garghoul plummet from view, then took a deep breath. He turned around and looked for the tunnel that he had taken on the way there. Then he stopped.

Emerging from the shadows, completely surrounding him, was an army of smoglodytes.

CHAPTER 6

RUMBLINGS

A DISTANT RUMBLING SOUND had put a constant frown on Magnus's liver-spotted and wrinkled face. From time to time, clanking, knocking, and rattling sounds echoed down the tunnels. A faint, smoky aroma hung in the air.

"The network is not happy," Magnus said, peering this way and that with his pale, sunken eyes.

After a long journey down a spiral staircase, the repair party had finally reached the bottom of the Monarch Fields shaft. It should have been a short trip in the rackety old iron lift, but that, like every other device down there, was on the blink.

"Not happy? How the dickens do you know

that?" asked Freddie Dove. "You're just trying to scare me."

"The tunnels speak to me," said Magnus, lurching off with sudden energy on his two walking sticks, like some humanoid insect. He scowled at a broken fungus globe. It was quite dead.

"Oh, the tunnels speak to you, do they?" Freddie gave a short laugh. "Of course they do!" As Magnus stalked by, Freddie's face took on an anxious expression. "Just my luck to be in the hands of this barmy old fossil," he muttered under his breath.

Sam appeared at Freddie's shoulder. Sam was shorter than the son of Lord Dove, but sturdier and broad, bulky in his dark duffel coat.

"Hey, that's my grandad you're talking about," Sam said. For a moment his eyes met Freddie's. "And you're right—he really is a daft old fossil." Sam grinned. "But there's no one who knows the network like him. I wouldn't like to get lost down here without him."

Sam gave the indignant Freddie a steady look that made the young lord squirm a little. "What's your claim to fame?" Sam asked. "You look like you wish you'd stopped home."

"Well," confessed Freddie, "I did think the

facilities would be better down here. Isn't there any central heating?"

Some of the engineers chuckled. "It's always tough on your first time down," one of them said.

"Hmm . . . another shattered fungus globe," Magnus remarked from farther down the tunnel. "Curious."

"What's curious about it?" asked Freddie. "They must have all blown up when the electrics blew a fuse down here. Result of the great battle and all that."

"Except," said Sam, "fungus globes are little ecosystems. They are alive and make their own bio-luminescent light. They don't blow up."

Some of the engineers had started to mutter and shine their flashlights around nervously. The dark-ness and strange noises were unsettling.

"I suppose a flash flood could have—hurrrgh—caused it." Magnus wheezed as his ancient lungs struggled for breath. "But there's no other sign of that having occurred. It's almost as if someone has been deliberately smashing them."

"Oh, dry up!" said Freddie.

A strange scraping sound—from somewhere not far away—made everyone look around.

"Tunnels still not happy," observed Sam.

"I'm going to check the control box at the lift shaft," said one of the engineers. "This way!"

Several of the men headed off down the tunnel. Magnus called them back.

"I wouldn't stray too far just yet," he called. "Keep together, lads!"

The group ignored him and marched off into the blackness.

"Oh, leave them," said Sam. "I'll get the portable generator running. I've had enough of this darkness already." He turned around, shining his flashlight this way and that. "That's funny."

Magnus glanced back at Sam.

"I'm sure I left the generator over there by the wall," Sam said. "Now it's gone."

"Gone?" Freddie gave a hollow laugh. "How can it be gone?"

Sam shone his flashlight high and low. "I don't know—but it is."

"This is all your fault!" one of the engineers grumbled at Freddie. "We were a party of twelve before you joined us. Now we're unlucky thirteen."

"Don't be ridiculous," snorted Freddie. Everyone fell silent, listening to the sporadic groans and clanks echoing around the tunnels.

Suddenly a blood-curdling cry echoed all around them.

"What was that?"

"It—it came from up there," Sam said. "Where those men were heading!"

A black shape, like a jungle creeper, lashed out at the flashlight in Sam's hand, dashing it to the ground with a crack. The corridor was plunged into pitch-blackness.

"What in the name of—?"

Sam's words were drowned out in screams and cries from all sides. Cold, prickly tentacles wrapped around him in the darkness.

CHAPTER 7

OLD FRIENDS

OU!"

A child-sized figure stood before Theo; its gray skin was mostly see-through, like a plastic bag, with thin bones and pumping body parts visible within. Its head, resembling a wizened turnip, showed a face that looked like a hurriedly made Halloween lantern. It wore a strange, twisted smile.

"Greetings, Theo," said the crooked little imp. "I am Skun, chief tracker of the Ilk tribe, noblest of the Smoglodyte peoples."

Theo's hands crackled with bright green fire that made the smoglodytes leap back, shield their eyes, and cringe.

"Skun!" Theo cried out. "I might have known you would be involved!"

Theo was too angry and upset to be afraid of the strange creatures. He also knew that one touch from him could blow them to smithereens.

"What's going on? Where's Chloe?"

Skun, alone of his ragged mob, did not cringe and tremble before Theo's power. He stood his ground, and to Theo's amazement, continued to smile.

"Your friend is one of the lucky ones," said Skun. "She is still alive."

"Alive?" Theo felt a chill in his heart. "What do you mean alive? Why shouldn't she be? What are you talking about?"

Theo pointed an angry finger at the smoglodyte, and it sprang nervously to the ceiling, where it stayed, like an upside-down spider, to continue the conversation.

"She has been taken by the terrible *unbogoglia*," Skun said. "If they wish to kill an enemy they do it quickly. But they also take humans down . . . below. We saw her pass—alive and struggling. They obviously had other plans for her."

"Plans? What do you mean? How do you know?"

Skun remained on the ceiling, where many of the smaller smogs had followed him.

"We don't know what they do. But we are forced to hide from the creatures. And when we hide we see them — taking humans."

One of the smaller smogs, Florn, looked out from behind Skun. "It's fun to hear the humans scream," she said. "But it's not safe to laugh."

Theo frowned. Skun flipped himself off the chamber roof and landed in front of Theo again.

"Perhaps now, you will not destroy us?" asked Florn, following Skun to the ground. She was little more than a mere smogling and stayed cowering behind him. Theo eyed the strange figures uneasily.

"What do you want?" he asked. "Why are you here?"

Skun gave a low, ungainly bow. "Most noble Theo Saint, Lord of the Underworld and Entirely Dreaded Candle Hand." He paused, peeking up at Theo for signs of approval at this courteous address. He didn't get any.

"Many and great," began Skun again, "are the ties of friendship between us."

Theo looked puzzled. "Friendship? I can remember you hunting me down and attacking my friends."

"Ah, yes!" Skun replied with another bow. "Immortal deeds — that will always be remembered."

"With horror," said Theo.

"With err . . . great horror," said Skun hurriedly. "Indeed. A time of legendary adventures! But alas, things are now not so jolly as they once were."

"What do you mean?"

"We are doomed!" blurted out little Florn from behind Skun.

"The unbogoglia are wiping us out," said Skun, gesturing at the ragged and rather young crew of smogs behind him. "They come from out of the walls, the tiniest crack in the floor. We try to hide from them, but they have . . . feelers—and eyes that can see around corners. They strike in darkness. They seek to drive us out of the network and make it their own."

"What do you know about them?" Theo asked. "Where do they come from? What does their name mean—unbogoglia?"

Skun drew himself up and steepled his sticklike fingers with an air of great knowledge. "Ah, yes. Unbogoglia is an old smog term. It means that we don't know what they are and we have no idea where they come from."

Theo's heart sank. *They don't know where Chloe is,* he realized. *I'm wasting my time.*

"Oh, great Candle Hand," Skun said, "dreadest of the dread. You are happy—very happy—

51

with our news that your friend is still alive?"

"Very happy," said Theo dully. He had no idea how long Chloe would remain that way. Skun clapped his hands together and grinned with delight.

"You will now be even happier," he said. "For we have a proposition for you."

"Yes?"

"On behalf of the smoglodyte people, I offer you the friendship of the foul murk." The smogs looked up at Theo with imploring eyes. "Join us—be our ally, our hero, our slayer of foes!"

At these words, Theo's heart sank further. He looked down at his hands, which were now flickering with just the palest glimmer of light. As his rage had died down, so his power had faded away. The shock of the last hour began to hit home. Suddenly he felt drained and miserable.

"I think I know where slaying these creatures would lead," he said. "They might kill Chloe for sure then!"

He looked from face to face, as they awaited his words. "I'm not a slayer of anything," Theo said. "I only want to find my friend—not start a war."

"A war!" said Skun with enthusiasm. "Yes, we must start a war! The Candle Hand will form a great and dreadful society with the smoglodytes! We will crash, smash, splatter all our foes!"

The smogs grew excited at these words and began to leap around the chamber echoing Skun's words.

"Crash, smash, splatter!"

"No!" Theo cried. "I am not going to use my powers to—to smash and splatter."

"Not even to help your friends?" Skun asked in a pathetic voice. "Your dear companions of old? I told you—we are being killed off!"

"Just like you once tried to kill my friends!" Theo exploded.

"Yes, but we didn't, did we?" Skun attempted a fresh smile. "We failed. And for that, you are in our debt. A debt of gratitude and friendship."

"No," said Theo, becoming confused.

"You," piped up Florn, "the great Candle Hand, could kill the creeping things, the things that steal humans and slaughter smogs—but you will not?"

Theo sighed. The anxious faces of the smoglodytes surrounded him, staring at him, awaiting his answer. He just wanted them all to go away.

"I do have a power," he said. "I—I've told this to the humans too, but I want to use it to make things better—to help people—not to hurt anyone—not even . . . creeping things," he trailed off.

"Then your answer," whined Florn pitifully, "is . . . no?"

Theo looked bleak. "I'm sorry, very sorry that the creatures are killing you. But I am not a warrior — or a slayer. I cannot join you in your war — so I have to say no."

Silence hung in the shadowy chamber.

"I'll take that as a yes," said Skun.

"Look out!" screeched one of the smallest smogs. "It's them!"

A black tentacle like a whiplash ripped into the party of smogs. At the same moment a shattering sound filled the air, as behind them the fungus globe was smashed by flailing tendrils. Darkness descended.

"Flee!"

Smogs sprang off in all directions, one ricocheting off the side of Theo's head.

Theo couldn't see a thing. He heard a horrible scream and was splashed by wet innards as one of the smogs exploded.

"No!"

Theo summoned all his power and raised his blazing green hands above his head. By the light of his own crackling energy, Theo glimpsed a sparkling, slimy shape vanishing into a crack in the wall. Next to the crack, he saw what looked like the shadow of a smoglodyte, weirdly stuck to the tunnel floor. The dark, imp-shaped smear stretched out, sizzling faintly. It was all that was left of one of the smoglings.

Theo turned round slowly and inspected the chamber by the light of his own burning hands. He was alone again. He turned and fled.

———

Theo hauled his tired body out of the hatch and found his way to the back entrance of the Condemned Cemetery. Brambles scratched his legs as he squeezed through the broken iron gate but he didn't care. As he walked home through the rows of headstones, he scoured the starry sky in vain for a bat-winged figure.

The lights of a police car flashed in Kensington Gore. Chloe was somewhere under the ground and Tristus had not returned. As Theo trudged up the steps of Empire Hall, a hunched, whiskery figure in a shabby coat stirred on a nearby park bench. The tramp rose suddenly and hurried towards Theo with quick, nervous steps. But when a tall police officer appeared at the doorway to let Theo in, the tramp turned and slunk away.

CHAPTER 8

PETS

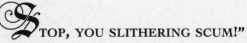

TOP, YOU SLITHERING SCUM!"

A voice cut through the darkness. The prickles withdrew from Sam's neck. Unseen creepers slipped off Magnus's throat. They heard footsteps as a group of figures drew nearer.

"Get away!" the voice cried. "The boss needs slaves, not corpses! How many times do I have to tell yer?"

A tiny gleam of light appeared in the tunnel. Sam and Magnus watched as a hulking figure could be seen, carrying a staff topped with a miniature fungus globe.

"Now what have we here?"

Sam blenched. He could now see that several members of the repair party were dead, sprawled in ugly postures like broken dolls on the tunnel floor. As Sam took in the scene, he glimpsed a black tendril, just as it whisked out of sight into the shadows.

The human arrivals were a ragged band, dressed in ill-fitting clothes that looked as if they had been rescued from a rubbish heap.

The tallest man drew closer. He had a great black beard, matted and thick with ash. Like the rest of the group of four men, he was caked in grime. His eyes were big and pale, slightly bulging, like those of a deep-sea creature. As he inspected Sam and Magnus in the gloom, he sniffed over them, more like an animal than a human being.

"Sewer Rats," breathed Magnus, leaning towards Sam. The acoustics of the tunnel, however, amplified the words.

Sewer Rats, Sewer Rats, Sewer Rats . . .

The bearded man turned to glower at Magnus.

"This one knows who we are," he said. "Very interestin'. Think we'll take him back to meet the master."

"Leave him alone," blurted out Sam before he could stop himself.

"Oho!" growled the bearded man. "And this one's not frightened." He peered closely at Sam. "The name's Hollister, by the way," he said. "And you—are my prisoners."

Sam tried not to cower before the man's gaze.

"If you ain't scared o' me," Hollister said, "you might be good enough to take a squiz at our little pets. Scare you right to death they will."

With a low chuckle Hollister gestured towards the dark shadows of the tunnel behind him. Among the dead bodies lying there, swirling tendrils could be seen and a strange glistening shimmer of half-glimpsed light.

"Your master?" Magnus asked, drawing himself up to his full height. "Who is master of the infernal creatures?"

"Infernal, 'e says." Hollister grinned, revealing several cracked and missing teeth. "Little darlin's they are, if you know how to bargain with them."

"Here's another alive one," a smaller Sewer Rat said from farther down the tunnel. He was a sallow figure, bald, with one eye that was permanently closed, looking rather like someone had stuck a hot poker in it.

"Show us 'im, Queasley," rumbled Hollister.

With surprising strength for his size, the one-eyed

Queasley hauled a human shape up from the floor. Whimpering, the body sank to the ground again.

"Mercy! Please!"

It was Freddie Dove. He was weeping like a child. It was now clear only six members of the expedition were still alive. The ones who had ignored Magnus's warning had borne the brunt of the attack.

"Pafetic!" cackled Queasley, throwing Freddie back against the wall. The young lord fell back to the ground, where dark tendrils curled around him.

"Are we ready, my pets?" Hollister growled. From the dark came a low hissing and bubbling sound.

"Take these survivors to the master," Hollister growled. Sam, Magnus, and Freddie were led away. Behind them, as their footsteps faded, dark tendrils emerged from the shadows and reached out for the fallen bodies.

CHAPTER 9

ORPHEUS

DESPITE HIS EXHAUSTION, Theo found it hard to sleep. Thoughts of Chloe's terrible disappearance haunted his dreams. And now and then he saw visions of the smoking body of the slaughtered smoglodyte. Sometimes he sprang awake, sitting bolt upright, convinced he had been woken by lightning . . . but he found himself sitting in darkness.

Is it my power?

Am I sensing danger, even in my sleep?

He lay staring at the ceiling. He didn't want to close his eyes. *Now I'm afraid to drop off, in case the bright light comes back.*

Or was it just a dream after all?

Gather your strength, Tristus had said. *Surely*, Theo thought, *I was right to go to bed. I couldn't stumble around those tunnels all night on my own!*

He had no one else to guide him now, so he decided he should follow the advice of the wise garghoul.

After hours of fitful dreams he looked at his clock: 5:45. It was morning now. Throughout his entire childhood he had been made to get up at this hour, to be given medicine he had never really needed, by a guardian who had never really cared for him. Even now it was hard for him to believe those bleak days were over.

Theo sprang out of bed and pulled on some warm clothes, including an enormous black sweater that Chloe had given him.

Tristus must have some news by now, but he can't speak to me if I'm indoors.

Putting on some boots, Theo stole out of the house, into the back garden, and out of the gate. This was the quickest route into the Condemned Cemetery—in fact it was the route he had taken the day he ran away from Dr. Saint.

A blue light was beginning to dawn. Shivering and breathing white clouds onto the chill air, he walked through the graveyard, searching the skies, the trees, and the rooftops of the mausoleums for a sight of the garghoul. But no pointed horns or jagged wings appeared against the sky.

Theo thought furiously.

Perhaps Tristus will return to the place where he left me. Theo remembered the chamber beneath the graveyard where they had spotted one of the creatures.

Should I go back there? Or wait for Sam and Magnus to return? He wondered how long they would be on their expedition. As he passed the cemetery keeper's cottage it looked dark, empty, and dead.

Still unsure of what to do, he went out the back gate of the cemetery, to the secret hatch that would take him into the network. Theo froze. Someone was there.

Police, Theo thought, glimpsing uniforms. The dark figures looked up and spotted him too.

He felt he had no choice but to draw nearer. The two men were wearing uniforms Theo had never seen before—of black leather, with polished boots and gloves. Each wore a little silver police badge, but of a kind Theo did not recognize. Both wore helmets with shiny visors that covered most of their faces.

"Good morning," Theo said politely. "Are you — searching the tunnels?"

One of the men loomed over Theo.

"What do you know about it? Who are you?"

"I'm Theo Wickland. I—I was with the police last night when, when—" his voice dried up. Suddenly he felt miserable and afraid. "You *are* police, aren't you?"

"Orpheus," said one of the men.

Theo frowned. "Orpheus, the ancient Greek musician?" he asked uncertainly. "The one who went down into the Underworld?" He had read about Orpheus in his book, *Greek Myths Retold for the Very Young.*

The two men looked at each other. "I think it really *is* him," one said.

"Yes," the other replied. "So much for all those reports of him vanishing into thin air yesterday!"

They looked back at Theo. "Orpheus is a new police division—a special force created by Commissioner Gold to battle this underground menace," one of the men said. "We'd better take you home, Master Wickland—you shouldn't be out."

"But—but I wanted to go into the network," Theo said. "I've got to— "

"Afraid not." One of the men shook his head. "No entry. The whole place is shut now. It's one big crime scene."

Crime scene? Theo supposed they were talking about Chloe being abducted. But there was something grim in their tone he couldn't quite understand. He gulped, fighting back a feeling of desperation.

"But—"

"The network is closed. No one goes in anymore unless they're Orpheus-cleared. Now—back home. And wait for police contact."

Theo followed, in gloomy resignation, as one of the men led him all the way back through the cemetery.

Theo climbed the steps of Empire Hall. It seemed to loom before him like a prison again. The Orpheus officer walked away, speaking into his radio. As the door closed on Theo, a tramp rose from a nearby bench and slowly approached the mansion.

Theo sat at the rather grand writing desk in his room, studying his precious map of the network. Magnus had made a copy of it, but this was the original. He gazed at its mysterious lines, color codes, and symbols. Somewhere down there—or beyond—was Chloe. Sam and Magnus were in the labyrinth too. How he wished he could be with his friends now.

Wait for police contact, he reminded himself.

But I am the Candle Man! Is waiting *all I can do?*

Just then, there was a polite tap at the door. "Breakfast, sir!"

Montmerency, the enormous butler, wheeled in a large cart piled with steaming silver pots and covered dishes. He plucked the lid off the main dish like a conjurer performing a trick.

"A Montmerency special," he said. "Eggs, pork sausage, kidneys, fried gammon, tomatoes, bubble and squeak, and black pudding. That'll put color in your cheeks, sir, not them bowls of birdseed Cook has been doing for you."

Theo eyed the mound of animal parts in front of him. Really, he preferred the birdseed.

"Thank you," he said flatly.

"By the way, sir," the butler said. "There's an old friend of yours outside — wants to have a word."

"A friend?" Theo's heart leapt. "Show him in!"

The butler's footsteps disappeared down the hall. Theo looked at his cooked breakfast warily. He broke a corner off a piece of toast and nibbled it.

A skinny, whiskered tramp came through the door. Theo's heart sank — he had been hoping to see Sam's cheery face.

"Good morning, sir," Theo said politely. He did

not wish to be rude. He had once heard tramps referred to as knights of the road, so he decided "Sir" was the safest form of address.

The tramp stopped a few feet away from Theo and gazed at him with ice-blue eyes.

"So at last we meet," the man said in a hushed voice.

"Oh, you!" said Theo. "I saw you in the street." He surveyed the stranger, who looked unkempt and gaunt, but not half as weathered and down-at-heel as he had expected a tramp to be.

"I know all about tramps," Theo said, feeling a little awkward. "Gentlemen of the open road. No worries, no cares. Whistling a merry tune as you swipe an apple from a passing orchard."

"I am not a tramp," the figure replied in wounded tones. "Do I look like I could whistle a merry tune?" He drew himself up indignantly. "I am Ex-Chief Benevolence of the Society of Good Works, ex-second-in-command only to the deceased Dr. Saint, the right honorable, Lord Timeus Dove."

Theo went white.

CHAPTER 10

DOVE OF PEACE

"ᴸORD DOVE?" THEO GASPED.

"The same," the stranger said. "I know much about you, Theobald. But owing to the extreme secrecy of our Society, we have, of course, never met. "

"B-But how — ?" Theo began to stammer. "I mean, why?"

The figure raised a finger to his lips. "Not so loud!" he said. "The police are everywhere. I've seen them stomping in and out of here all hours, looking through Dr. Saint's old files and records. There seems to be a constable at every door."

"Well, the police are here to protect me from

people like you!" said Theo, starting to take off his gloves.

He has returned, Theo remembered. Lord Dove had been missing since Dr. Saint's defeat. Was this his new archenemy?

"Stop!" hissed Lord Dove, backing towards the door. "You don't need protecting from me anymore. Much as I hate it, you're the head of my Society!"

Theo kept his distance.

"But I always heard that you were an immaculately dressed man — even more so than Dr. Saint," Theo said, puzzled at Lord Dove's scruffy appearance. "Mr. Nicely told me about your white suit and lilac gloves."

"I've been on the run," Lord Dove snapped. "Hiding in tunnels, flitting from one wretched hole to another, like a fox." He looked affronted. "Anyway," he added, "to avoid capture I have to appear as little like myself as possible!"

Theo thought about this. "Oh, yes," he said, the cleverness of this strategy hitting him. "That's rather good! But why have you come? And how did you get in?"

"Under a word of truce. Rapscallion," he said. "Your staff had to let me in. It's old Society rules.

Luckily your butler used to work for one of our old members, Baron Patience."

Theo looked puzzled. Lord Dove shut the door quietly. He approached Theo again, step by cautious step. Mr. Nicely had once told Theo that there was nothing so dangerous as a cornered rat. Well, Lord Dove was something like a cornered mouse.

"It's—it's my son," Lord Dove said.

"Freddie?"

"Yes. My only son, Frederick. May I have a spot of coffee?" he asked suddenly, eyeing a round silver pot on Theo's tray.

"Go ahead," said Theo. "But I thought the Society of Good Works regarded coffee as poison: the *Brown Death*."

"Ah, yes," sighed Lord Dove, rather shakily pouring himself a cup. "While Dr. Saint was alive we had to follow rather a lot of beliefs. Times have changed now, haven't they?" he added. "Perhaps a little bit of death can be good for you."

This reckless attitude shocked Theo quite as much as Lord Dove popping up from the park in the garb of a tramp.

Lord Dove went pale and somber again. He continued in a low voice. "Last night a work party went down into the network. A group of thirteen."

"I know," said Theo. "I waved them off."

"Half were found dead this morning."

"Dead?" Theo felt a chill pass through him. He stared stupidly at his visitor, waiting for more.

"I may be on the run, but I have a very efficient spying network in place. I monitor police communications. The rest of the work party appear to have escaped—and are now somewhere in the network." Lord Dove continued, "The survivors—as far as we know—include two of your friends . . . and my sole son and heir, Frederick."

Theo felt weak—but also giddy with relief. Whatever terrible thing had happened, his friends had escaped it.

"Why—why have you come to me?" Theo asked.

"I want you to help find my son," Lord Dove said. "He is obviously in terrible danger. Every second could count. But the police"—he suddenly looked exhausted and bitter—"the police are shutting down every known way into the network."

"Yes," said Theo. "They stopped me going in earlier."

"There are terrible creatures on the loose down there," Lord Dove said. "I've heard police reports—"

"I know," interrupted Theo. He did not want to mention Chloe. "I—I've seen them. I destroyed one last night."

"Destroyed one!" Lord Dove exclaimed with excitement. "Yes, there . . . I knew you could do it! I knew I should come to you."

For a moment it seemed to Theo that Lord Dove gazed at him with a look of awe.

"But what can I do?" Theo asked.

"You're the Candle Man," Lord Dove said. "There are things you can do that no one else can. In the Society we've all heard rumors of the old stories. If half of what we've heard is true, then . . ." His words faltered, as if he dared not give voice to his hopes.

A strange, desolate feeling welled up inside Theo. "If I'm so special, then why did you all try to kill me?" he asked bluntly. He tried to look tough, but inside he was quaking with emotion.

"Dr. Saint poisoned our minds against you," Lord Dove said. "He said the Wickland blood made you wild, uncontrollable. He said your power had to be contained, siphoned off, and used without your knowing."

Theo felt almost overcome with rage and misery for his wasted childhood of lies and captivity. For a moment he felt as if he could hardly stand. Taking a deep breath, he supported himself, leaning against a chair.

"Can I have one of those sausages?" Lord Dove

asked suddenly. Theo was glad for the distraction, glad not to be held by that glassy stare.

"You see," said Lord Dove, "we didn't know that our dear kind leader was secretly planning to be the Candle Man himself."

Theo nodded. Lord Dove took some toast.

"I haven't eaten for thirty-six hours," he said through a big mouthful. Theo wasn't surprised to hear that Lord Dove was starving. He knew from all his storybooks that bad men didn't prosper, and not getting to eat much was the least he expected them to suffer.

Theo felt off-balance. Suddenly he remembered Chloe—how he wished that she were there to advise him! She would say it was bad tradecraft to let an enemy eat your breakfast or something clever like that.

"So tell me," said Theo. "What can I do?"

Lord Dove jumped up as a heavy tread sounded at the door.

"Rapscallion," said a lowered voice. It was Montmerency. "I think the time might be right, sir," he said. "I would get moving if I were you."

"All right," said Lord Dove. He turned back to Theo. "So will you help? If I give you the means to enter the network, will you go?"

Theo nodded. Freddie Dove was with Sam and Magnus. They were all survivors together. Anything Theo could do to help Freddie would also benefit his friends. It might also — Theo hardly dared to hope — lead him towards Chloe.

Lord Dove leant forwards. A little nerve was quivering under the haggard man's left eye.

"Do you have the seal of the Society of Good Works?" Lord Dove asked.

Theo nodded. The Society's solicitor, Mr. Sunder, had made it clear Theo should keep the seal secret and near to him at all times. Theo had already used it once or twice, making documents official by pressing its symbol into wax.

Lord Dove now looked very nervous. Theo awaited what he had to say. He had the feeling that a lot depended on what Lord Dove was about to ask. The whiskery face drew nearer to him.

"And have the police said anything to you about the icehouse?"

"No."

"Then let me show you a little secret."

CHAPTER 11

THE CAPSULE

"WHERE ARE WE?" Sam whispered.

Darkness was all around them. The prisoners were exhausted after a long march down a series of broken stone stairways and winding tunnels. Every step of the way, thorny tendrils had slithered over their feet and around their ankles, reminding them of their peril. Now they had stopped on the edge of a big black crater, the rim of which could just be made out, due to a faint glow from within.

The air was full of drifting fumes. The distant rumble and clank of machinery reverberated all around them.

"Judging from the acoustics," Magnus said, "my guess as to our location—" Here he stopped and gasped for air, his eyes bulging. "Hurrrgh!"

Magnus opened and shut his mouth like a drowning goldfish.

"Great Scott," Freddie Dove gasped. "He's going to drop dead!"

Sam slapped Magnus on the back.

"No, he's not," Sam said. "Magnus always does this. His eloquence is too long for his wind. Keep it short, eh, Grandad?"

The prisoners fell silent as one of the Sewer Rats walked by, then disappeared down a stairway into the crater. Sam went to peer down after him, but a tendril pulled him back sharply.

"Don't annoy them, you idiot!" Freddie snapped.

"I was going to say," whispered Magnus, "that I believe we have now reached the bottom of the Well Chamber, the great cavern where Dr. Saint performed his experiments."

Sam looked puzzled. "But—but I thought all this was destroyed in the big battle."

Magnus nodded. "The great alchemical explosion did destroy the mechanical contrivances of the Well Chamber, but—*hurrrgh*—they appear to have awoken something else . . . underneath. There are old Society legends," he added, ending with a deep frown and silence.

"Go on," said Sam. "Don't stop there!"

"I don't want to worry you," said Magnus.

"For Pete's sake!" Sam exploded. "What could be more worrying than you saying 'I don't want to worry you'?"

"Silence!" bellowed Hollister, the enormous Sewer Rat chief.

"The mysteries must be respected," muttered Magnus, lapsing into silence.

"But Grandad—arrrgh!" Sam cried out as he received a blow to the head from Hollister's wooden staff. The great, bearded brute glowered at the captives, then descended into the crater.

"That'll learn yer," the one-eyed Queasley snickered in passing. The Sewer Rats went ahead, leaving the prisoners alone again.

"Yes," whispered Freddie after a moment. "Shut up, Sam, for goodness' sake. Didn't your secret society teach you to whisper quietly when trapped by bloodthirsty maniacs? It's on page one in my book!"

"Ow!" Sam fingered a bruise arising on his head. "Who are these charmers, anyway?"

"They are Sewer Rats," said Magnus. "Rogue Foundlings and assorted villains who have made these tunnels their home. They formed themselves into a gang many—*hurrrgh*—years ago." Magnus reached into the pocket of his long brown coat, pulled out a little brown bottle, then stuffed it into his nose and breathed deeply.

"That's better," he croaked. "Hollister's their leader. He's the worst of the lot—a bully," Magnus said. "Occasionally, this gang of pirates used to do a bit of dirty work for Dr. Saint—I've spotted them on my monitors."

Sam winced as a stinging tendril tugged at his leg, urging him to move. The captives were shoved towards the crater by one of the Sewer Rats.

"Rest's over," shouted Hollister, appearing again with a cracked grin on his ash-smeared face. "The boss is ready to see you now!"

A narrow staircase wound down the walls of the crater. The prisoners stumbled through a thick, foul-smelling darkness, lit by a faint fiery glow ahead. Finally, dry-mouthed and with stinging eyes, they emerged into an enormous cavern. How far it stretched could only be left to the imagination. Its jagged roof could be glimpsed in the fitful fires that spat and glowed from an enormous stone building that loomed before them.

The vast stone construction rose up and filled the

cavern, in great steps, like the immense temple of some lost religion. Except there was one difference; This temple was dominated by an enormous chimney that rose like the cone of a volcano, far up into the dark vault of the roof.

A couple of guards, armed with long rifles, greeted Hollister and the party of prisoners. Hollister turned, his eyes gleaming.

"More fuel," he growled gleefully, "for the Furnace!"

"Suppose they see us," Theo whispered. He was standing in the courtyard garden, a chilly breeze plucking at his coat.

"We'll be safe for now," Lord Dove replied. "Montmerency is taking care of the police that were hanging around."

Theo went pale.

"With doughnuts," added Lord Dove. "My own recipe. Sugar is a subtle weapon in my hands. I had Montmerency pretend that the cook made too many. Doughnuts will keep any guardian of the law occupied."

Lord Dove raked with his foot through the frosty mulch of decayed leaves that covered the ground behind the old Memorial. A drain cover appeared.

"Entrance to the old icehouse. Great mansions had these before fridges were invented. Rumor has it that the key to this store was lost long ago."

Lord Dove took the seal from Theo and knelt down. "But rumor can be manipulated." He twisted the head of the seal into a socket in the drain cover. With a delicate exhalation of air, the circular cover rose. He glanced around nervously.

"In! Quickly!"

Theo felt a moment of panic at following Lord Dove inside. Could he trust this man? But his anxiety for his friends overcame him. They descended by some thick stone steps. Of course, it wasn't an icehouse at all, but a small, circular chamber. Control panels gleamed in the half-light. The room was dominated by an upright, man-sized silver tube with a sliding door.

"Over the years, the head of the Society of Good Works has had his own private means of entering the network," Lord Dove said. "This will take you straight down to the bottom."

Lord Dove pressed a button and the door slid open.

"You could be in the heart of the network in no

time at all. Find out what you can, then come back. You might even get lucky and find . . . find some-one." Lord Dove did not name his son again, but Theo could see the worry in the man's eyes.

"Would—would you be coming too?" Theo eyed the machine doubtfully. It reminded him of the hated Mercy Tube his guardian had used to steal his power.

"The mechanism will only take one," Lord Dove said, scrutinizing the capsule. "It is designed for secrecy and speed. You have the diabolical powers—I do not!"

"Did Dr. Saint build it?" Theo asked.

"No, a far more arrogant mind conceived it. A mind that could imagine needing no other help but his own—Erasmus Fontaine, the original Philan-thropist. Now that you are the head of the Society, his inventions are yours."

Theo's mind was racing. Was he doing the right thing?

"Take a careful look at the diagram," Lord Dove said, pointing to a yellowing chart on the wall. It was covered with a spidery collection of ink lines. Theo was intrigued to discover another rendering of the intriguing realm beneath his feet.

"Drawn by the Philanthropist himself. Now pay

attention—this whole mission will fail miserably if you make a wrong step."

Lord Dove said this as if making a wrong step would probably come naturally to Theo. Theo scoured the map with eager eyes.

"Don't get out at Level One—it's not deep enough. That's where all the basic secret passages are. You probably know a few already."

Theo nodded. He had used those several times—usually with Chloe as a guide.

"Level Two is the next. Again: avoid. Smelly canals and blue mosquitoes. These tunnels are pretty wrecked now, cracked and flooded." Lord Dove gave Theo a cold look. All of that damage was a result of Theo fighting against the plans of the old leader, Dr. Saint.

Now Lord Dove pointed to a large oval shape in the next section down.

"Level Three. This is where you get out. The Well Chamber is here, the center of all the alchemical technology. Communications are best here, decent tunnels, fungus globes. You'll be close to where those survivors might be." His voice quavered for a moment.

Theo frowned as the scribbled lines became more vague below Level Three.

"What's down here?" asked Theo. "Level Four? It's all pretty unclear on the map I've got."

"Ignore those levels. They're an environmental hazard—ash pits, heaps of waste. I wouldn't go there if I was paid. And Level Five is empty caverns as far as I know. Probably overrun with foul creatures. Avoid like the plague."

Theo's heart was pounding. He moved over to the shining silver tube that seemed to be beckoning him inside.

"How does this work?" he asked, stalling for time. He stepped gingerly onto the threshold of the machine.

"It's weight activated!" cried Lord Dove. A transparent doorway shot across the opening, knocking Theo into the capsule. A light flashed. A thrumming noise started.

"Stop it!" cried Theo. "I—haven't decided yet!"

"I can't stop it!" Lord Dove shouted. "Go to Level Three!"

Theo grimaced. Three was his unlucky number. He pressed the button, but a light immediately flashed for Level Four.

"It—it's saying Level Four!" Theo shouted. An unnerving clicking was going on above his head.

"Not Level Four!" shrieked Lord Dove. "Don't go to Level Four—or Five!"

A red panel lit up. There was a sudden explosion and Theo rocketed in the capsule, far below the earth.

LEVEL FIVE

𝕿HE CAPSULE DID NOT STOP at Level Three. Theo studied the controls with growing alarm. The number four glowed obstinately instead. With an ear-splitting sound, the capsule was redirected. It sped down a new tube, deeper into the heart of the network.

The Well Chamber must be more badly damaged than Lord Dove realized. The capsule can't stop there. Some sort of emergency-override system must have kicked in. So what happens now?

The capsule reached Level Four. And passed it.

Theo gulped. *We're heading straight down to Level Five.*

He gave up being brave and closed his eyes. *My powers*, he told himself, *my powers will look after me. Please.*

Like a torpedo, the capsule shot downwards through the darkness. Theo closed his eyes. A sickening plunging sensation was followed by a loud klaxon blast and then a great whoosh of air. Buffeted by powerful turbulence outside, the silver tube slowed down, then stopped with a jolt. Theo's stomach felt like it had turned right over.

Silence followed, except for the low clicking of the machinery, now at rest. Theo waited for something disastrous to happen. Nothing did. Instead, the door slid open, and cool air flowed in. A sense of relief flooded over him as he stepped out into a gleaming silver control room, a carbon copy of the one in the icehouse.

I've landed in one piece, Theo thought, trying to stay calm. *I might be on the wrong level but at least I can start looking for my friends.* He opened the door of the terminus and peered outside. A huge dark cavern stretched before him, lit here and there by patches of bioluminescent fungus.

Shadowy fears threatened to overwhelm Theo's mind.

Don't panic, he told himself. *You are the Candle Man. The Candle Man will find a way in the darkness.*

Theo sat down on some rocks and unfolded his precious network map. He studied it intently, but tiny lights were dancing before his eyes. Theo blinked and shook his head, but the lights did not go away.

He peered more closely into the darkness. A chill ran down his spine. Slithering forms crept and bubbled all around him, their barely glimpsed bodies reflecting flashes of light from the glowing fungus.

Theo was surrounded by the creatures that had taken Chloe.

He peered at them with fascination. Any normal person might have been paralyzed by terror. But Theo had not been brought up as a normal person. Surrounded by fairy stories and fanciful picture books all his life, Theo knew little of what passed for normality. Being surrounded by a horde of monsters in a subterranean chamber was scarcely more unusual to him than bumping into boys playing football in the park.

That was why he did something that had never occurred to any of these creatures' victims: he spoke to them.

"How do you do," said Theo awkwardly. "I,

um . . . I need to talk you. It's very urgent. There's been a terrible — mistake."

The creatures flexed and bubbled in the darkness. They looked rather like jellyfish, with an outer rim of extendable feelers. They were very flat, several feet across, and some of them had eyes that rose and blinked on stalks.

"You — you took my friend. Or some creatures like you did. I think that it must have been a mistake. . . ."

Theo desperately hoped it was. There was a pause. Then one of the creatures lashed out with a feeler. It whipped painfully around Theo's leg and tiny prickles bit into him.

Theo cried out with pain. A shiver of excitement went through the slimy horde of twenty or so. Theo used his teeth to bite into one of his gauntlets and tear it off. Before he could take any further action he was jerked into the middle of the vile, slurping bodies. He felt a jelly-like lip suck at his ankle. Blood was trickling from his leg.

"That's enough!" he shouted. He summoned all his anger and plunged his right hand into the middle of the nearest creature.

Fwoom! It went up in a column of blue flame, emitting a ghostly shriek and shedding burnt fragments of feeler across its comrades. Where the ashes fell, the creatures screeched, howled, wailed, and slithered away into the gloom.

Now Theo stood, smeared with ash and slime, in a circle of clear ground, with the creeping things seething a respectful distance away from him.

"No!" came a thin, unearthly voice. "Do not fighting us."

A tingle shot up Theo's spine at the sound. For a moment he forgot his peril and stood in awe.

"You—you can speak!" Theo said. Suddenly he felt more optimistic. If these things could talk, then they could think—respond to reason.

"Allow me to introduce myself," he said, strictly following the formulas he had been taught at Empire Hall. "My name is Theo Wickland." Then, he added, "Some people know me as the Candle Man." He raised a still-smoking hand with streaks of ash on it.

The creatures pulsed in the darkness, as if pondering their reply.

"We are the crelp," one of them said. "Do not fighting with us—for we—we only wish to killing of you, as is our custom."

The unearthly frankness of this left Theo stunned.

"Why do you want to kill me?" he asked.

The crelp seethed again, fluttering and squelching in the dark.

"Because dead is better for humans. Better for us—for what we wanting to do," came a low, eerie reply.

Theo frowned as the circle of crelp seemed to edge nearer to him.

"Do not attack me, or I *will* fight you," Theo said in as polite a way as possible. "We seem to have gotten off on the wrong foot," he added. Then he remembered that the crelp didn't have feet. *Another gaffe.*

"You—um . . . speak very well," Theo said.

"We can speaking your tongue because we have taken some humans inside of us," a crelp said. "We absorb you, so now we can talking with you. Please let us eat Theo."

"No!"

Theo held up his hand; it burned with green fire. The creatures withdrew nervously.

"Are there people—like me, down here?" Theo asked. "Are there other humans? Your—your kind took one . . . by mistake, called Chloe."

The crelp bubbled and fluttered the edges of their jelly-like skins in the darkness. Theo could hear noises like hissing and spitting as if the creatures were arguing among themselves. Finally, one creature slithered nearer to Theo.

"You do not hurting us again?" asked the creature. Theo frowned.

"Only if—if you're good," he said. "And answer my question."

"Then the crelp will taking you to special place."

"What place?"

"Follow. We will take you to our secret larder."

CHAPTER 13

THE MAN WITH NO FACE

THE FURNACES," CROAKED MAGNUS, gazing up at the smoking edifice before them. "I never thought to set eyes upon them."

The fires from the great building illuminated the scene in sudden bursts like the lightning from a brooding storm.

Some great and sinister work was at hand. From tunnels in the rock wall, coal trucks were arriving. Slaves in ragged clothes operated a giant turntable that received the trucks, emptied their load down a chute, then turned the trucks around, back into the caves.

"If the Great Furnace is working again—then at

least part of the legend is true," Magnus breathed.

The prisoners looked up through the fumes, as a dark figure emerged from a doorway in the Furnace and began to descend a stairway towards them. The slithering creatures scattered as he approached, as if repelled by loathing — or fear.

"What legend?" asked Sam.

"Mr. Norrowmore knew the tales," Magnus said sadly. "Our old leader, now gone. He spoke of the Great Furnace and the Wonderful Machines that lay below. Power enough to rip a world apart. I — I didn't listen. I told him that those days — those fears — were over."

"What fears?"

"Shut it!"

Sam was smashed to the floor by the gnarled staff of Hollister. As soon as he hit the ground, he was covered in black, stinging tendrils.

"No!"

A commanding voice, so cracked and hoarse it was painful to hear, tore through the air. Its owner gestured towards Sam and a sudden blast of searing flame sent the creatures slithering and hissing into the shadows.

"Only I decide life and death down here," the figure rasped.

The prisoners looked in disbelief at the man who had spoken. A dark figure with smoking hands, cloaked like some ancient warlock, towered over the cringing Sewer Rats. As they gazed at the one who reigned over all in this terrible place, the truth slowly dawned on them.

The man had no face.

His head was one great mass of charred flesh, a grotesque, ash-gray scar. No hair, no features remained, just two deep-set, glimmering eyes, the slightest crack for nostrils, and a twisted gash for a mouth.

Sam glanced towards Magnus and saw that his grandad was staring, transfixed.

"Dr. Pyre!" Magnus breathed at last. "It—it cannot be!"

"We saved these intruders into your kingdom, to be used as slaves," Hollister said to the faceless man. "But some of 'em won't learn to shut up!"

"The people who never learn are usually the clever ones," said the faceless man in his ravaged, deep voice. From their dark hollows, two glistening eyes looked upon the new captives.

"Can we have them for the ash tunnel?" asked Hollister. "The slaves there are dropping like flies."

The faceless man considered for a moment.

"The ash tunnel, then," he said.

As the slaves were led away, the rasping voice spoke again. "Not this one!"

Dr. Pyre walked slowly towards Magnus, who had stayed rooted to the spot, staring, thunderstruck.

The faceless man turned on his heel and gestured towards some crelp guards.

"Bring him. The old man will come with me!"

CHAPTER 14

THE LARDER

"WOW—WHAT IS THIS?"

Following the crelp, Theo had emerged from a narrow tunnel onto a high gallery of rock.

Stretching out below, Theo could see a series of long mounds curving away into the depths of the cavern. At first, he thought it was a spectacular rock formation, but it slowly dawned on him that the whole thing was manmade. The long, low hills were in fact giant underground pipes. Covered with a fine layer of dust, they blended into the natural beauty of the cavern.

"It's like I'm seeing the earth's plumbing," said Theo. "What are these pipes for?"

The crelp hissed amongst themselves.

"The crelp don't knowing that," one of the creatures said. "And the crelp don't—what is the word for it—we don't care."

Theo was fascinated by this evidence of some gigantic scheme of building work that went far below the city.

"But you live down here—you must know something."

"The crelp do—are not living down here. Not usually. Our kind—many, many—are living in the darkness of the Chasm. A horror place—horrid."

"So what are you doing here?" Theo asked. "Creeping around, attacking people. You won't make many friends that way."

There was something almost childish about the crelp that made Theo want to scold them.

"The crelp don't wanting to make friends," one of the creatures hissed. "We are only being here because we were released from the darkness."

"Released?" Theo echoed. "How? By who?"

The crelp bubbled and hissed for a while among themselves.

"It is not worthy—worthwhile—crelp telling you. We will probably tricking you soon and make you die. It is better."

Theo frowned.

The crelp are wicked and innocent at the same time, he thought. *Perhaps I can get through to them.*

"The crelp should be more friendly," Theo said firmly. "You should answer questions and tell people things." He continued to follow the creatures as they slithered along the rock gallery towards a stone arch ahead. "That's more polite. Don't you have any manners down here? You are doing terrible things now, things that we, on the surface, don't do at all."

Several of the crelp surrounded Theo for a moment, gliding on their feelers in an almost dance-like fashion.

"The crelp liking doing terrible things," one said. "We were a long time in the darkness with only each other to feed on. Now we have—having—new ones to kill and eat—it is very nice."

Theo frowned. A thought suddenly occurred to him. "And why are you taking bones out of grave-yards? That's something else we don't do."

The crelp gave a long crackling hiss that was almost a nasty laugh. "We have other plans, Human Theo. More horrible. Too horrible to tell, but very nice for us."

Theo sighed. The crelp really were hopeless.

As he reached the end of the rock gallery, Theo began to lose sight of the enormous pipes.

"I wonder if those pipes connect up somehow to the alchemical city in the Well Chamber?" he mused. The crelp simmered with discontent as he pulled out the crumpled network map and pondered it.

"The rocket capsule sent me down to Level Five, here," he murmured. "The Well Chamber is Level Three, so these pipes aren't actually shown on the map. Unless . . ."

Theo gasped. There were faint, pink marks that appeared all around the map, occasional details appearing to link them to a mysterious section in the unexplored Level Four.

"Unless the pipes are indicated by the pink outline—in which case they are utterly, stupendously enormous. . . ."

"This way, this way," urged the crelp. "It doesn't matter. Theo dead soon, won't care about it."

Theo hurried after the crelp. He felt ashamed. *It's a very great fault of mine that I find maps and diagrams so interesting*, he chided himself, *when I'm supposed to be rescuing my friends.*

"Now you will be our friend," the crelp said. "Here is the larder."

At first, Theo saw nothing. Then as his gaze

followed the path of the crelp, he began to make out
a curious stone dwelling, a refuge with a single
narrow door and no windows, cunningly built into a
natural cleft in the cavern wall. It looked like some
ancient secret hideaway—or prison.

Theo approached cautiously, but there seemed to
be no sign of life.

"You will open it," one of the crelp said. Several
feelers probed helplessly at the door, but it was too
tightly sealed to allow even those insidious creatures
any way in.

Why do they call it the larder? Theo wondered. A
nasty suspicion dawned in his mind.

"Look," said Theo. Several eyes sprouted up
around him on jelly-like stalks, as if the crelp
were only too keen to do so. "You're supposed to
be helping me—I want to know if you've seen any
other humans down here—"

Theo stopped. He thought he had heard a movement beyond the closed door. He bent his head
closer to listen.

"Is—is there someone there?" called a voice.

Theo stood back, astonished. His heart almost
exploded with joy and relief.

"Chloe!" he cried out.

"Theo? Is that you?"

The crelp were seething excitedly around Theo's feet and he had to kick one of them away.

"Are you a prisoner?" Theo asked. "Can you get out?"

Before a reply could come, the crelp interrupted.

"Human Theo, you—you will open the larder for us?"

Theo ignored this.

"Where are the creatures?" Chloe shouted.

"It's all right," said Theo. "There's been a mistake." He looked down at the crelp. "A mistake, right?"

"Yes, yes," the crelp agreed eagerly. "Mistake, Theo, mistake!"

"If the creatures have gone—get me out!" Chloe said, unable to tell what was going on outside.

Theo studied the door. There was a strange stone carving, a half-moon shape, in a recess by the door.

"I'm locked in here," Chloe shouted.

Theo pondered. Then he raised his hand and placed it on the half-moon shape that appeared to be a kind of lock.

The rare energy inside me: the tripudon power. It can melt things, but it can also cause changes, Theo thought. *Perhaps a tiny spark . . .*

Theo had never tried to use his power on something like this before. He concentrated, pressed the half-moon symbol, and attempted to summon up the mysterious tripudon fire.

Nothing happened.

"Come on, Theo, I've been stuck here all night!"

The anxiety in Chloe's voice seemed to kindle something inside Theo. Suddenly his fingers sparked. The half-moon symbol glowed and sank inwards. There was the harsh *clack* of a hidden lock. The door was open.

"Thank you," said the crelp.

Suddenly a pack of seething jelly-forms rushed at the door and started to squeeze into the crack, forcing it wider.

"No!" screamed Theo.

The crelp paid no attention. "Now we feed," they cried. "Later, we harvest the bones!"

"It *was* a mistake," another crelp screeched. "Mistake to let her get inside and escape us."

Theo whirled around, facing the bubbling horde. "No!" he screamed.

CHAPTER 15

REFUGE

T HEO TOUCHED THE LEADING CRELP just before it could force its way through the door.

Thwoom! It disappeared in a streak of blue smoke. Thorny creepers tugged at Theo's legs and hauled him over. He smashed his forehead against a rock and started to bleed.

"Theo!"

He could hear Chloe crying out. The crelp were getting in.

Fwoom! Blam! Boom! Theo lashed out wildly at every crelp he could get his hands on. He struggled back to the door through smoking, wailing, exploding pools of jelly.

102

He hurled himself through the half-open door, turned around, and slammed it shut. He leant against the door, breathing heavily. Outside, everything had gone quiet.

"I—think it's all right," Theo panted.

Chloe was there, her hair dirty and ruffled, her big navy blue coat torn, with a pocket hanging off, her face drawn and pale.

"Nice use of 'all right,'" Chloe said with a smile. "We're trapped beneath the ground, surrounded by flesh-eating monsters, and—"

"And what?"

"And I've never been so pleased to see you in my life! But wait—you're hurt."

Only now did Theo realize that warm blood was trickling down his face. Chloe studied the wound, her head cocked to one side.

"Gory looking, but not serious," she said brightly. "Kind of suits you."

Theo smiled. "Does it?"

"No, of course not," said Chloe. "I'm just trying to make you feel better, you twit. We'd better bandage it up."

Theo smiled again. It was great to have Chloe back.

Chloe tore a sleeve off the pale blue shirt she was

wearing and tied it around Theo's head. She admired the finished effect.

"A real wounded hero." She grinned.

"But what happened to you?" Theo asked. "How did you end up in here?"

Chloe sat down on a stone ledge. Theo peered around. They seemed to be in some ancient work-room or lab.

"An old alchemist's refuge by the looks of it," Chloe said. "It may even have belonged to the original Philanthropist. Make yourself at home."

Theo looked at the rows of clay pots along the shelves. Many of the walls had ancient symbols scratched into them. There was even a pump of some kind and a water basin.

"The crelp snatched me from that graveyard," Chloe said, "dragged me down to these caves, and then they started to argue amongst themselves. They were torn between taking me to be a slave or eating me. They were very up front about it, though. Refreshingly frank."

"They are!" said Theo with a sudden smile. "Mostly. Except they've got some horrible secret, they said — some plan too nasty to tell."

"Great," groaned Chloe, rolling her eyes. "It gets

better! Anyway, they had just decided to eat me, when your friend the garghoul dropped by. Seems he had been tracking them. Tristus swooped down and carried me to this refuge, where they couldn't get at me. Then he said he needed to fly to the source of the problem straightaway and couldn't take me with him."

"So did he talk to you?" Theo asked.

"Not exactly. Apparently garghouls are very picky about who they communicate with. He kind of muttered things mysteriously and flew off. Well, I'm used to being treated like that — being in a secret society with Magnus. Anyway, Mr. Tristus said he'd come back for me." Chloe looked tired now, and anxious. "But he never did."

"He said the same to me too," Theo said. "I hope he's all right."

"Oh, he'll be all right," she said. "They're made of stone, aren't they? What I really want to know is how the incredible Candle Man came and saved me!"

Theo suddenly felt ten feet tall. He related his tale, patiently answering Chloe's barrage of questions. She frowned deeply when she learned how Sam and Magnus had disappeared.

"Basically, nobody is safe with these crelp things

running around," Chloe remarked. "As I said—they either eat you, or drag you off to be a slave."

"A slave for who? For what?"

"Find out that and I'm guessing we'll find Sam and Magnus," Chloe said. "Did you get all of them?" she asked suddenly.

"I hope so."

"Well, we can't hide in here forever. Let's take a look."

Theo opened the refuge door and led the way out, his hands aglow, ready for the first sign of a tentacled enemy. Dead crelp lay smoldering and bubbling around the entrance, but no living creatures were to be seen.

"Where are we going?" asked Theo.

"Into danger, of course," Chloe said, her glance darting from side to side as she left the refuge. "Stay vigilant!"

———————

"Bring him!"

The faceless figure, tall and dark, in ragged garb, sat in his command chair, surrounded by control panels, pistons, and gear wheels: the gleaming instruments of ancient alchemy. Wisps of black smoke curled up from cracks in his ashen skin. In that ghastly head, deep, dark sockets showed a glint of moist eyeballs.

"I want the old man—now!" rasped the broken, painful voice. Two thorny, aged crelp seethed and fluttered their tendrils at his feet.

From the doorway emerged Queasley, the one-eyed Sewer Rat, prodding Magnus with his staff. The old cemetery keeper heaved his bony frame along, on his two walking sticks. With grim resolution the old man navigated his way slowly through the glittering dials, spinning iron wheels, and screeching pressure valves that filled this, the top of the central tower in the Great Furnace.

The control center had no roof and was open to the airs of the cavern, and the giant chimney, built of immense stone blocks, towered above them in the darkness, belching stinking smoke. Flecks of ash danced in the air and rained down on the shining control stations, but no one seemed to care.

Hollister and Queasley, staffs in hand, flanked Magnus as he was presented to their master.

Magnus gazed at the faceless man, still struck with disbelief.

"Dr. Pyre," he breathed. "How can you be here . . . now? You died, many, many years ago!"

The faceless man's eyes flickered, as if they might

spontaneously combust at any moment and take his whole head up in a grisly bonfire.

"It appears not," he growled. He paused. A far-away look came over his ravaged features. For a moment his harsh voice sank to a whisper. "These are strange days indeed," he began. "To the denizens of this underworld, the slinking smoglodytes and the sly garghouls, the whole human era is known as the *After Time*. They speak as if our whole age is but an afterthought of creation. Well, it seems that Dr. Pyre, too, has been allowed After Time."

Magnus gave the ashen man a deep, penetrating look, as if searching for something only he could see.

"What year is it?" Dr. Pyre asked suddenly.

Magnus told him. The faceless man nodded.

"I see," he said in a strange, soft tone that seemed filled with sadness.

"But master, why do you believe him—and not us?" asked Queasley. "We found you in the tunnels, we're the ones who follow you!"

"Because," Dr. Pyre roared suddenly, "this is a world of lies!"

Dr. Pyre cupped his hand and let a small fire crackle there. "This is a world that deserves to burn."

The two Sewer Rats laughed coldly at this and raised their staffs in salute at the sentiment.

"Back in the old days—the ones you now call Victorian," Dr. Pyre said, "we used to say that when a man bought a newspaper, the only truth it reliably contained was the date on the front page."

Queasley nodded. "Yes, yes—very good, sir!"

Dr. Pyre peered darkly into the distance. "Now even that verity has lost all meaning for me!"

Hollister and Queasley exchanged a look, uneasy.

"Time means nothing down here, master," Queasley said with a cracked smile. "Survival comes by seconds, not years."

Silence followed, punctuated by the rumblings of the Furnace.

"A world of lies," said Magnus, musingly, edging closer to Dr. Pyre on his battered old sticks. "Indeed. Well, I know of a good lie. A lie that sits before me."

Queasley and Hollister stepped back, as if expecting Magnus to be incinerated on the spot. To their surprise, Dr. Pyre merely laughed.

"I know your secret," Magnus said calmly.

Dr. Pyre suddenly arose, shedding fragments of his ashy skin.

"Enough!" he shouted. "All the secrets will burn now, and my great enemy will burn with them."

The smoldering man gestured at the gleaming technology around him.

"Behold, the Wonderful Machines," he said. "As large as life, and not a mere shadow of legend. I have a final, brilliant task for them, to purge and purify this world."

He advanced on Magnus.

"I need a wiser, older head, to help me when I go into the vault below to start up these ancient devices. You will serve me."

Magnus gave Dr. Pyre a long look. "No," he said.

Dr. Pyre's eyes glowed. Dark smoke curled from the cracks in his skin. He seemed about to burst into flame.

"You *will* serve me!" he repeated.

"No," repeated Magnus calmly. "And, as you can see," he added, "I am far too old to be scared—even of you."

Smoldering, and shedding the occasional spark, Dr. Pyre glowered at the cemetery keeper. Finally, he turned away.

"Then I shall proceed, alone," Dr. Pyre snapped. "Without delay."

He strode off angrily, ashen skin cascading from his body, as he headed for the doorway.

Hollister looked puzzled.

"What—what shall we do with the old man?" he called out.

"Take him," Dr. Pyre muttered, "to the deepest dungeon."

PHASE TWO

*D*ID YOU HEAR THAT?"

Theo looked around uneasily. He and Chloe were winding their way up a spiral staircase, hewn into the rock behind the fortress.

A rumbling sound echoed down the stairway, from above.

"Vibrations, shaking the whole place," Chloe said. "I think I know why."

Theo forced his aching legs to keep pushing, taking him higher up in the darkness. He almost tripped over Chloe, who was crouched, waiting for him where the stairs ended.

"Keep down," she whispered, waiting for him. "There might be guards."

"Guards guarding what?" Theo asked. "Where are you taking me?"

Chloe beckoned Theo to follow her through the stalagmites to a gap in the wall ahead. As Theo neared, he could see it was an arched and ornamented doorway, linking the stairway to a cavern.

And the cavern was enormous.

"Level Four," Chloe breathed. "The crelp argued about bringing me up here—to their boss. So of course, we have to take a look."

Far away, through the darkness, a vast building loomed, like a nightmarish factory. A towering, monolithic chimney spewed black smoke high into the cavern roof. Lights flickered through the fumes, from a row of guard towers. Fires flared from beyond the Furnace's fortress-like walls.

"What is it?" gasped Theo.

"It's enemy action," said Chloe, staring into the distance. "When those crelp were arguing about what to do with me, they kept talking about their master."

Theo looked across at the fiery edifice with awe.

"It seems he's the one who started up this ancient furnace," Chloe continued. "He's the one who released the crelp, and I'm guessing he's the one who's captured Sam and Magnus."

Theo gulped.

"So that's where we're going," Chloe said finally.

Suddenly she bent down and started to rub ash into her face. "Do what I'm doing. It's important to blend in."

Theo pulled a face. Throughout his childhood, Dr. Saint had never let him get dirty at all. Even now, it was hard to defy his upbringing.

He had lost his gloves in the battle at the refuge, cast aside and mired somewhere in a slick of smoking crelp slime. Now he crouched down gingerly, poked his finger into the ground, and with great daring dabbed a tiny smudge of ash on the end of his nose.

"It won't kill you," said Chloe. "But being seen might."

Theo grabbed a handful of soot, shut his eyes, and made sure his face was thoroughly filthy.

Chloe grinned. "Now you look like a real boy."

Theo grinned back. It was nice having Chloe there to tell him what to do. He was used to being given orders and he felt more at home now with Chloe taking charge.

"I always wondered what was on this level," said Theo, staring ahead towards the Furnace. To his eyes it looked like the dark realm of some fairy-tale underworld king. "It's amazing!"

"It's terrible," Chloe said, her face looking grim and resolute in the volcanic light from the distant fires. They set off across the cavern, their feet slipping and sinking in the mounds of ash that coated the floor.

"There are tales, legends from years ago about this place. I can remember our old leader, Mr. Norrowmore, talking about them when I was just a little girl."

Theo's ears pricked up. Mr. Norrowmore was the legendary leader of the Society of Unrelenting Vigilance. His recent death had left the secret society in disarray.

"So you knew him back then?" Theo asked, giving Chloe a curious glance. "Did Mr. Norrowmore look after you?"

Chloe shook her head. "Society members don't talk about their pasts," she said with a superior air. "The mysteries must be respected."

Disappointed, Theo plodded on through the ash. Chloe looked at him and her face softened.

"Well," she sighed, "remember my mum died when I was young. My sister Clarice went into a Society of Good Works orphanage, but I was adopted by a couple of Vigilance agents. For reasons of secrecy I'll call them the Weird family. Mr.

Norrowmore would come round to visit them sometimes. Late at night he would sit around with Mr.
and Mrs. Weird discussing the old myths of the
Society—always when they thought little Chloe was
fast asleep—"

"Aha!" Theo interrupted brightly. "So your real
name is Chloe Weird."

"No, you clot! Anyway, you're off the point. One
night I heard them all yarning about some inventions, buried deep in the network: the Wonderful
Machines. They were built in an age when
alchemists conjured with power beyond our under-
standing. Mr. Norrowmore said they could rip a
hole in the world."

Theo gulped. He wanted to ask Chloe if she
was exaggerating but somehow couldn't find the
courage.

The sight of the smoking furnace seemed to swim
before Theo's eyes. Why did things that looked so
wonderful have to be terrible too? A deep foreboding
began to grip him as he plodded on in the fiery
light. Now and then the clanking of underground
machines seemed to shake the very rock around
them. After one particularly loud boom, a stalactite
plummeted down from the cavern roof above and
landed in the ash only yards away from them.

"Nice places we go together," Chloe said, giving Theo a smile.

"Hey—look!"

Theo pointed towards the Furnace. On the top of an ash heap, human slaves could be seen, carrying heavy sacks. As they trudged closer, more and more dark figures became apparent, toiling away under the watchful eyes of the crelp.

"We should try to get close to some of these prisoners," Chloe said. "Ask them a few questions!"

Clang, clang, clang.

A high-pitched sound rang out through the air.

"Dinnertime," Theo said.

Chloe gave him a withering look. "Dinnertime?"

"Well, it's like the special gong at Empire Hall— when important visitors came to dinner." Theo looked glum. "Not that I ever saw any of them," he added.

"Sounds like an alarm to me," Chloe said. "Don't tell me we've been spotted!"

Clang, clang, clang. The noise was getting louder, more insistent. Theo noticed that many of the workers had downed tools. People started shouting and running.

Then it happened.

The ground shuddered. Chloe fell over and cried

out, as the ashes burnt into her hands. A deep groaning noise filled the air. A red light blazed from the main tower of the Furnace.

"Get out of here, you idiots!" someone shouted, racing past them in filthy rags. "Don't you know it's Phase Two?"

"They think we're slaves, as well," Theo said. "The alarm isn't about us!"

"Something's up!" Chloe said. "We'd better—"

She stopped, as with a deafening rumble, the ground beneath their feet trembled and began to shift.

"An earthquake!" exclaimed Theo. He had read about them in books but never expected to actually be in one.

"Come on!" Chloe tugged at Theo's sleeve, but he stood transfixed, watching the ground break up into gigantic cracks.

"This is no earthquake!" cried Chloe. The cracks were not random, jagged shapes but perfectly straight lines. Ash cascaded down into the darkness below as the cavern floor split up into huge plates.

With a thunderous groaning that sounded like the end of the world, the giant plates started to retreat into the cavern walls. Everywhere slaves were racing towards the edge of the cavern.

Clang, clang, clang. The alarm rang out over the deafening screech of machinery. Chloe shoved Theo forwards as the very ground they were standing on began to disappear beneath their feet. Chloe stumbled and screamed.

"Run!"

CHAPTER 17

MOSS BREAK

THEY STOOD ON THE LEDGE, Theo gasping for breath and coughing on cinder dust. Chloe gazed into the black hole that had opened up at their feet. The ground, which had been an artificial surface, concealed under layers of ash, had now been withdrawn into the cavern walls.

"Well, what a bit of luck," panted Chloe. "We arrived at showtime!"

With the cavern floor gone, the Furnace stood now, like a dark fortress on the edge of an abyss. They had made it into one of the many tunnels that surrounded the cavern, and from the edge they had a perfect view of the yawning chasm below.

"Phase Two," Theo said. "Making a big hole." He looked puzzled.

But as they stared downwards, tiny points of light appeared in the shadowy gulf.

"Look!" said Theo excitedly. "There—and there!"

The abyss was coming to life. Far below, lights began to shine, tiny pinpricks at first. Slowly, shapes began to appear in the gloom—great wheels of silver, spires of glass, and enormous pistons, as tall as great trees. Theo could only stare, awe-struck. It was like a whole city of marvels beneath their feet.

"The Wonderful Machines," breathed Chloe.

"Hey, you two!"

Theo jumped as a voice echoed out of the cave behind them. A one-eyed man in filthy rags waved a staff at them.

"Get back inside, you two," the figure snapped. "Before I belt yer!"

"Human guards! The plot thickens," whispered Chloe.

"Pathetic specimens," the guard muttered. "Don't know what the crelp were thinking of, bringing you two."

Behind the man's back Theo and Chloe exchanged a hopeful look. They had obviously been taken for slaves who had gone astray. With his bandaged head and ash-smeared face, Theo was certainly unrecognizable as the young master of Empire Hall.

"Join the others—get some water. Wait for orders." Queasley waved regally with his staff, sending Theo and Chloe farther down the cave.

"Who was he?" hissed Theo.

"Looked like a Sewer Rat to me," Chloe said, making sure she couldn't be heard. "Those tunnel pirates I told you about. Looks like they're mixed up in something big this time. Whatever you do, don't let on who you are! Keep your head down and let me do the talking."

Suddenly they emerged into a smooth, manmade tunnel. Ahead, a dim fungus globe illuminated a startling scene. In a circular chamber, a row of slaves were lining up to drink water from a pool. The exhausted figures were so caked in ash it was impossible to tell them apart. A guard with a staff stood by the pool to make sure there was no dawdling.

"Do what I do," Chloe whispered, quickly joining the line for water.

Theo drank thirstily when offered the bowl.

"Don't guzzle too much," said the guard with an unpleasant snicker. "They say it turns you into one of them!" His glance flitted towards a passing crelp, its translucent body almost invisible in the half-light.

This remark seemed to intrigue Theo, but Chloe nudged him along forcefully before he could reply.

"Over there," she urged. She steered Theo towards the darkest corner of the chamber, where a couple of slaves were resting.

"Well, well, well," Chloe said, "what have we here?"

Sitting on a rock, covered head to toe with ash, and looking very sorry for themselves, were Sam and Freddie Dove.

Sam's soot-caked face split in a grin of pure delight.

"Theo!" Sam gasped, jumping up. "Chloe!"

"Sit down, you twit!" hissed Chloe. "And for goodness' sake, shut up!"

The guard glanced vaguely towards them, then continued dishing out water for some new arrivals.

"Well, it's about time," Freddie said without enthusiasm. He glanced at the guards that surrounded them on all sides. He also looked meaningfully at Theo's bandaged head. "What kind of a rescue do you call this?" he added.

Sam was still beaming.

"You're miracle workers, you two!" he whispered. "How did you get in? How did you know we were here?"

"This isn't a rescue—yet," Chloe said quietly, sitting down on a rock and adopting the gloomy, downtrodden air of the other slaves. "It's a Vigilance Reconnaissance mission," she added. "Grade three," she added randomly with a glance at Freddie. Then she frowned at Theo, who was gawping around the chamber like a tourist.

"Slump a bit," she urged Theo with a shove. "Fit in. Look like you've been working hard."

This left Theo a bit bewildered, as he had never really worked hard in his life. He studied the slaves around him, who slouched despondently with heads down, hands and arms in stiff postures, cramped with fatigue. Copying as best he could, he took a perch next to Chloe.

Theo quickly explained how they had made it there. Freddie frowned at the story of how Lord Dove had implored Theo to find his son.

"I thought the old villain hated me," Freddie said with a doubtful air. "Must be going soft in his old age."

"Where's Magnus?" Chloe asked.

"Alive," Sam replied. "As far as we know. He was taken away somewhere else. I suppose he was too old for this kind of work." Sam tried to sound cheerful, but Theo could tell he was deeply anxious.

"Okay—Magnus is tough," Chloe said. "We'll worry about him in a minute. First of all, what's going on down here?"

"This is the ash tunnel," Sam said. "We've been slaving down here, scraping burnt waste away from the furnaces. There's a whole load of different heat chambers."

"It's awful," Freddie said. "Back-breaking work and only cave water and a bowl of moss at tea break." He poked the foul sludge in the bowl on his lap. "No doubt this is rather a treat for Sam, but I expect my seven courses when it's nosebag time."

Chloe gave a patient smile. "I'm talking big picture," she said. "It looks like someone is trying to get some ancient alchemy working. Something big. Have you seen the boss?"

Sam clouded over. "A menace from the Victorian age," he said. "Dr. Pyre."

Chloe started. She looked shocked for a moment but swiftly covered it up.

"We've seen him," Freddie whispered. "He hasn't got a face. Just that head-shaped, burnt scab. Horrible."

Theo gulped. "Is he on my list of enemies?" he asked Chloe.

"Oh, yes," said Chloe quietly.

125

Freddie picked up a pinch of feathery moss from his bowl and sniffed it. "He would be on anyone's list of enemies," he said, "according to the legends of my Society."

Freddie popped the spinach-colored morsel into his mouth and made a face.

"Go on," Theo urged.

"Quietly and in a bored voice," advised Chloe, glancing around.

"Back in the Victorian days there was the Candle Man and there was the Philanthropist, and people had to take sides, for one or the other."

Theo felt a special tingle crawl up his spine. He loved, and yet feared tales about his formidable ancestor.

"Except, Dr. Pyre was different. He was against everybody. He had crazy ideas—a philosophy, he called it. Hated the world, apparently. What they call a nihilist. He wanted to tear creation down and start again. A prize nutter."

Sam swigged his cracked beaker of filthy water. "But how did he get that . . . that face?"

"My father—back when I was a nipper and he still had time to talk to me, said Dr. Pyre saw himself as a rival to the great Philanthropist. Wanted to be master of the elements."

"You mean he's another alchemist?" Theo was scared but intrigued.

Freddie nodded and beckoned them closer. He seemed to be enjoying the attention. "He gained some kind of control over fire—but at a terrible cost. Ended up a walking pile of cinders. The Incinerated Man, the newspapers called him."

"But how—?" Sam frowned. "How can he still be alive now?"

"Blame it on Lord Wickland, the original Candle Man," Freddie said with a bitter smile and a meaningful look in Theo's direction. "According to the legends of the Society of Good Works, not everyone the Candle Man touched was melted. His power was unpredictable. Some of his enemies were transfigured—doomed to act out their madness forever."

Theo nodded. That fit with some of the things he had discovered in his adventures. One of Lord Wickland's enemies, the Dodo, had been turned into an immortal by the Candle Man's touch. Theo shivered. Now he had inherited the same terrible power—and its consequences.

"But why is Dr. Pyre firing up this old furnace?" Theo asked. "What's he up to?"

"You don't know the power of this place," Freddie

said. "According to our legends, there are . . . machines down here—built in ancient days. It's bad news—for all of us."

"Told you." Chloe glanced at Theo. "The Wonderful Machines."

Freddie nodded. "If Dr. Pyre wants to burn down the world and start again," he said with a sudden tremor in his voice, "well, these machines might just give him the power to do that."

"Cheerful pair, aren't they?" Sam commented.

Theo wanted to say something to cheer Sam up but he couldn't think of anything. He puzzled over his old problem of how—and where—to deliver an encouraging pat on the back, then gave up.

Clang, clang, clang.

The distant gong sounded once more. Freddie sprang to his feet, knocking his bowl to the floor. "Phase Two must be finished," he said. "Look, they're sending people back to work."

Sewer Rats had started to urge slaves back to their feet. Theo and the others rose slowly.

"We'll have to get back to the raking station, or there'll be trouble," Freddie said, trying to drag Sam away.

"But what are we going to do?" Theo asked.

"You have got to get out of here," Sam said with a

determined look. "Go and get help. This is too big for just the Society of Unrelenting Vigilance. Theo, even you can't beat this lot on your own. There's old No-face, then there's the crelp, and on top of that these underground thugs called the Sewer Rats," he added.

"Dr. Pyre was the bane of the original Candle Man," said Freddie darkly. "According to Society legends, old No-face was the one your famous ancestor never defeated. His last enemy."

Theo looked to Chloe for confirmation. She nodded. Freddie was eager to carry on.

"Some say he—"

"All right," snapped Chloe. "I think we've had enough yarns for one day." She threw a quick glance at Theo.

"I think this is worth telling!" Freddie snapped back. He gave Chloe a shrewd gaze. "And I think you know it already!"

"Now isn't the time," Chloe insisted.

"You people and your secrets!" Freddie exclaimed. "You're as bad as my father!"

Theo interrupted. "Tell me—tell me about Dr. Pyre," Theo said. "I—I want to know."

"I only wanted to say," Freddie sighed, looking warily across at Chloe, "that it rather looks like Dr.

Pyre was the one who finally blew out the original Candle Man."

Theo gulped.

Suddenly Sam cried out as a sharp tentacle snatched at his ankle. While they had been talking, a crelp had slithered up behind them.

"Get a move on!" yelled Queasley. Insistent pulling and prickling from spiny tentacles forced them all to get up and head down the tunnel. Theo and Chloe exchanged anxious glances. If ever they were going to be exposed as intruders it was now.

"Right," said Chloe quickly, "here's what we do—"

"Silence!"

The bellowing of a harsh voice made them all stop. Striding towards them, through the ranks of Sewer Rat guards, was an imperious, cloaked figure.

It's him, Theo thought, his insides quaking. *The one who blew out the first Candle Man.*

The ashen head, that hideous ball of cauterized scars, tuned towards Theo and Chloe.

"These will do," Dr. Pyre growled. "Bring them!"

CHAPTER 18

THE FOOL

"THESE ONES?" The giant form of Hollister, the chief Sewer Rat, peered down at Theo with a puzzled frown. He sniffed him, like a wary rodent, and frowned. "I don't remember the crelp bringing 'em in."

"There's a lot you don't notice, Sewer Rat," Dr. Pyre snapped. The faceless man studied Theo and Chloe again. "This feeble pair are useless to me as workers," Dr. Pyre said, "but perfect for a special task I have in mind. Now get the others back to work."

Through his soot-crusted fringe, Theo peered at the man he was doomed to call his enemy, even though he had never met him before, never personally angered him. Theo stared at that dark blot of a head, the glimmering pits of eyes, the cracked and crusted skin, gray like the scarred-over surface of a dormant volcano. Was this the last sight the original Candle Man had ever seen?

"Get down there," Hollister snarled, pointing Theo towards a narrow tunnel that branched off from the chamber. Theo kept his head down. Trying to act the part of an obedient slave, he walked between two crelp guards towards the tunnel.

"Stop!"

Theo froze in his tracks at the voice of Dr. Pyre. He heard two heavy feet crunching through the ash behind him.

"What is your name?" the harsh voice demanded. Theo's heart pounded. He stared fearfully at his hands.

Not now, he told them. *Don't glow now. He must not know who I am.*

His heart was pounding.

"I—I . . ." Theo's mind went blank. He was terrified and simply didn't know what to say.

"No matter," rumbled Dr. Pyre. "Henceforth, you shall be known in my realm as Fool!"

The faceless man peered at Theo curiously,

eyeing the bandage around his head, the ash-smeared face.

"All my other slaves avoid the murdering crelp like the plague," he breathed. Theo could see into those eyes now, strangely bright and liquid amidst that dry, ashen ball of a face.

"Yet you, Fool, choose to take a shortcut through them!"

Theo closed his eyes, wishing himself miles away. What an idiot he had been. Of course, all the other slaves kept away from the vicious crelp as much as possible. But Theo had already spoken to them, defeated a whole horde of them. Deep down he didn't have the same fear of the creatures that every other slave had. Now, his lack of fear had made him stand out—the last thing he wanted.

In his anxiety, Theo fell back on the ways of his cloistered upbringing. He gave a little, deferential bow, the kind his antique *Book of Manners* recommended when addressing someone of superior standing. It occurred to Theo that the faceless man was a doctor after all.

"I—I'm sorry, sir," he said. "If it was impolite of me—not to be afraid."

There was silence. Dr. Pyre glowered at him. Then he made a curious unearthly noise, a wheezing, gasping sound that turned into a raucous cackle.

Theo realized with astonishment — Dr. Pyre was laughing.

"Impolite?" The man roared again and the strange laughter changed into a terrible racking cough.

"The Fool talks of manners when he stands on the edge of doom," Dr. Pyre muttered. He groaned and bent over in pain, the unexpected outburst of laughter had hurt him.

"Get going, Fool!" he said. "Your good manners will be the death of me!"

Relieved beyond words, Theo trudged on into the tunnel.

"Nice work," muttered Freddie to Sam. "I hardly think Dr. Pyre noticed him at all."

Theo heard Sam cry out, as Hollister landed a nasty kick on him.

"Quit gawping, you — and back to the ash tunnel!"

Sam gave Theo a hopeless look as he and Freddie were taken back towards the Furnace.

Dr. Pyre strode to follow Theo, bringing Chloe with him. Crelp shadowed Chloe's every step.

"To the Crypt," roared Dr. Pyre.

The stairway spiraled down into blackness. The ancient stonework was slippery with water leeching through the rocks. Dr. Pyre was somewhere behind them, out of sight. Crelp guards straggled ahead.

"What's the Crypt?" Theo asked Chloe in a whisper.

Crypt, crypt, crypt . . . the echoes of Theo's voice whispered around him as if they had a life of their own.

Chloe turned and put her finger sharply to her lips. Before disappearing into the darkness ahead, she made a motion that was either a shrug or a shudder.

We have to get away, Theo thought. *I can't fight this Dr. Pyre—not if he defeated the original Candle Man. That would be just throwing my life away. I have to get back to the surface—tell the police what's going on.*

They finally emerged from the stairway into a lower tunnel. It was damp and smelly, filled with puddles and pools in the rocks. Dr. Pyre's fiery glow reflected and danced in the mirroring pools around him.

Exhausted after the long descent, Theo bent over, his hands on his knees as he tried to catch his breath. All the ash he had inhaled made him feel sick.

By the light of Dr. Pyre's smoldering form, Theo could make out some details of the tunnel they were now in. Glancing up, he could see the long, smooth curve of one of the great pipes he had seen earlier, when he had been traveling with the crelp. It curled along the top of the ridge above, before vanishing into darkness. Dr. Pyre was taking them — by a different route — close to the caverns where his adventure had started.

"This is bad," Chloe added. "We want to get farther up — so we can slip away to the surface — not farther down."

Theo gave her a faint smile. "Remember my story of how I got down here?" he said. "There is a way back up — that only the head of the Society of Good Works knows about."

Chloe shushed Theo, nodding towards their sinister guide. He was standing before a stone doorway, studying it with great interest. Fire flared from his hands as he touched the door here and there, as if inspecting it.

Theo could see there were fine lines and symbols carved into the stone.

"You see," came a thin, troubled voice. The crelp had massed around the door and were quivering. "The doorway is closed. We telling — told you. A something has happened—very bad. You promised the crelp we can be free."

Dr. Pyre glowered. "Don't fling my promises at me, you inhuman filth," he said, but fire flickered through the cracks in his skin, and he seemed disturbed. "This place is old. The Crypt has—it has ideas of its own," the faceless man said, more to himself than the creatures. "The doorway may have closed by some ancient design."

Dr. Pyre placed his hand on a round shape in the center of the door. As he did, a spiral of little dots glowed into life. The door began to slide open.

"Reports came today of more police," he muttered, "more spies in the tunnels above. I want you creatures to rise upwards and flood those passages. Choke them with your tentacles and your rage. Let no one through."

The crelp assented with an excited sizzling sound.

"It's the police that must be stopped—at all costs," Dr. Pyre said.

"Free more of our kind," begged the crelp, "and we will letting no human into the network—that, we promise!"

"When my work is done," Dr. Pyre said, "the crelp can have these tunnels to live in, forever. I, for one, will be finished with this world."

The crelp gave a satisfied hiss and seethed around the foot of the gate. Suddenly the faceless man looked across the tunnel towards Theo and Chloe.

"Come, my Fool," he said, "and your friend. Fate has brought you to me."

"What—what do you want us to do?" Theo asked nervously.

"I want you to come with me, to a place where few mortal men have ever set foot. You will serve me . . . as my canaries."

Bewildered and afraid, Theo stepped into the dark.

CHAPTER 19

CANARIES

THE STAIRWAY DOWN towards the Crypt was narrow, slippery, and so dark Theo had to feel his way along the damp walls.

"Why are we leading the way?" Theo asked. "We don't know where we're going!"

"Good question," muttered Chloe darkly.

At least the air was clean here, Theo thought. He took a deep breath, but it was damp and chilled the heart.

Behind them the slurping of crelp guards and the heavy tread of Dr. Pyre was magnified by the stone tunnels. With the far-off dripping of pools and the occasional shifting and settling of rocks, the cavern sounded full of restless, unhappy life.

"Why does he want us as canaries?" Theo asked Chloe. "Does he expect us to sing?"

"Not exactly . . . ," Chloe started to reply.

"You obviously know nothing of the mining industry." Dr. Pyre's voice echoed eerily down the passage, as if he were speaking from everywhere at once. "Miners take caged canaries with them as they work beneath the ground. If poisonous gases lurk nearby, the little birds will reveal that by dying first."

"Is there poison gas down here?" Theo asked in alarm.

"No," Dr. Pyre answered, his words echoing all around. "But there are evil spirits—malign powers—which can prove just as deadly."

Now Theo and Chloe emerged onto a metal platform built into the rock. The cave suddenly opened into a cathedral-like vault of extravagant limestone shapes.

"Beautiful," Theo said quietly.

Dr. Pyre stood beside him.

"I chose you well, Fool," he muttered. "One of the most dangerous places on earth, and you admire its beauty."

"Why is it dangerous?" Theo asked.

"You are in the Crypt," the faceless man growled.

"This is the secret that has given birth to all the other secrets."

"What—what do you mean?"

"There is a crack in the world," Dr. Pyre continued. "A crack beneath London. It is a way through to another realm—an underworld of creatures that do not belong in our age."

Chloe was still standing as if frozen. Theo reached out a hand to grab her arm. She paid no attention.

"This is where they all come through," the faceless man croaked. "The smoglodytes, the garghouls, and worse. That is why I need my canaries."

"Oh, I see!" Chloe's voice suddenly rang out around the cavern. It was filled with an unexpected delight. Theo looked on in surprise as she turned to face him. By the eerie glow of Dr. Pyre's smoldering form, he saw her eyes were bright and she was smiling.

"Thank goodness!" Chloe cried.

"Are—are you all right?" Theo asked.

"All right?" Chloe laughed. "I've never been better."

There was something fixed about her smile—like the grin on a portrait, or a waxwork, thought Theo. He felt puzzled at first, but soon the happy feeling seemed to spread over him too.

Chloe took Theo by the arm and led him forwards.

"It's okay, Theo. I understand now," she said. "I thought this was a dangerous place. But now that I'm here I can sense only . . . kindness."

"Kindness?" Theo sighed with relief.

Dr. Pyre loomed behind them. "Kindness," he muttered. "Ah, yes, of course."

Theo grinned back at Dr. Pyre. Now he, too, was full of the happiness that Chloe felt.

"You were wrong, sir!" he said, grinning up at the faceless man. "There might have been monsters down here once, but now I can sense . . . friends!"

Theo spun around with a gleeful abandon he had never felt before. It was all clear to him. Coming to this crypt had been his destiny. His whole life had been leading up to this moment. Now he would be truly happy.

His eyes scanned the forest of stalagmites all around for signs of life. Suddenly he expected to see happy smoglodytes, kind garghouls, playful phantoms in the shadows.

"They're hiding," he laughed. "Shall we go and find them? Shall we make friends?"

"Oh, yes," Chloe cried back, breaking into a skipping run. For a moment it struck Theo oddly—he had never seen Chloe skip before. But the misgiving soon vanished. It was going to be wonderful to meet his new friends. He could sense them waiting for him just ahead.

They tripped eagerly down the stairway, towards the welcoming darkness below.

"No!"

Dr. Pyre's roar seemed to shake the cavern. With a swift gesture he blocked the path ahead with a wall of flames. Dr. Pyre grabbed each of them with a biting, clawlike hand on the shoulder.

"Stay," he growled.

Theo blinked in the sudden glare. "Why did you do that?" he cried.

Dr. Pyre peered silently beyond the crackling wall of flames. "There is no happiness here," the man whispered at last. "Step slowly forwards."

Dr. Pyre waved a hand and the wall of flames disappeared. He held up one hand like a glowing torch. Just ahead, where Theo and Chloe had been about to run, was a concealed pit. With a gesture, Dr. Pyre illuminated its depths. Deadly pointed stalagmites could be glimpsed far below.

All the happy feeling drained out of Theo. He sank to his knees. Chloe gave a short cry and slumped next to him.

"Ah, my canaries," growled Dr. Pyre. "You have served your purpose well."

In his faint, red glow, Theo and Chloe clutched each other. Theo peered anxiously into Chloe's eyes to check that his friend had come back to her usual self. She gave him a slight nod.

"The attack comes differently every time," Dr. Pyre said. "From the evil powers that lurk down here. Sometimes through illusion, sometimes through fear, the dark forces seek to catch mortals unaware. This time, through the realm of hopes and desires they have come, invading your hearts and stealing away your minds!" He surveyed Theo and Chloe with his deep, liquid eyes.

"If I had not brought two weaker minds with me, as an early warning, then I may well have been deceived. I could have stepped into the trap."

With his fiery hand he revealed a way around the pit. He pushed past Theo and Chloe, leaving them to struggle after him.

"The attack has failed," Dr. Pyre said. "We may proceed. From now on, I shall lead the way."

Theo stumbled on. He now felt a great emptiness inside. But his mind was his own again. Chloe patted him on the arm and gave him an abashed smile.

"Forces of darkness," she said. "They get you every time."

Theo smiled, then felt the crelp tug at his ankles with those familiar thorny tendrils.

Dr. Pyre led them into the heart of the Crypt, down a ringing iron stairway bolted into the rock. Far below, tiny lights were winking through a ghostly mist.

As they descended farther, Theo could make out the shape of an enormous gateway rising from the cavern floor below. It was like a great prison wall stretching across the center of the cave, barbed with spikes and glittering with warning lights.

"This is it, my dear Fool," Dr. Pyre said. "The secret at the heart of the Crypt."

Dr. Pyre peered through the mists and cast one or two flares down into the gloom, but they revealed nothing.

"This is where the crack in the world is hidden, known to a select few as the Chasm. This is where it all comes from—the nightmares, the shadows, the things we do not understand. Like the crelp," he added significantly. "In ancient times, the alchemists built this great gateway to hold back the horrors. Some have the gift of opening it."

"But now it is closed," the crelp hissed. "Something

is wrong—our kind come—coming through no more!"

"Indeed," Dr. Pyre said. "Something has barred the way, and that must be rectified. We will descend. My canaries will remain here."

Theo and Chloe were left on the last iron platform before the descent to the great gate. One thorny, immense old crelp was left to guard them. It sat, a long way up the steps above them, silent, almost as if sleeping.

Dr. Pyre disappeared down the stairs into the mists, followed by the other crelp. Chloe nudged Theo.

"Time we were going," she whispered.

Theo wondered if he could defeat that hideous, sprawling crelp. He began to summon his power.

"Well?" Chloe urged.

"Yes," came a clear, soft voice.

In a blur of motion a black shape dropped from the ceiling and drove a broken stalagmite clear through the center of the crelp guard. The creature stiffened, thrashed its tendrils wildly, then became still. Theo looked on, wide-eyed.

Tristus had come to their rescue.

As Theo gazed in delight and relief, the garghoul fell to one knee, then collapsed facedown on the floor.

CHAPTER 20

SPIES

RISTUS!"

The garghoul began to rise up from the floor of the platform. Theo could see that the creature's stony skin was scored and scratched with terrible marks. One of his claws was broken and one of his wings was horribly ripped, flapping at an awkward angle. A chip had splintered away from one of his horns.

The garghoul's eyes burned a pale blue. "You must flee," Tristus said. "I tried to keep you away from this peril, but it seems destiny is stronger than the will of an asraghoul."

"What happened?"

"I followed the crelp—I found your friend and tried to keep her from harm." He nodded politely towards Chloe, who gave a slight bow in return.

"I tracked their evil to here—the gateway. They were pouring out of this place. There was a battle— I managed to kill all of the ones in this crypt, then closed the doorway with an ancient asraghoul word of command."

At that moment, wild screeching sounds echoed up from the mists below. It seemed the crelp had discovered their fallen comrades.

"I . . . I was too injured, too weak to leave this place," Tristus said, slowly clambering up onto two feet. "I was forced to enter my stone dream to recover my strength. But now that you have arrived down here, it seems my work is not done."

"You have to get away with us," Theo said. "You're too hurt to take on Dr. Pyre."

At the mention of this name, Tristus looked grim.

"There are things here that you do not under-stand, Theo," he said. "Now leave quickly."

With a grimace, the garghoul rose into the air awkwardly, with one broken wing.

"Tristus!" Theo cried. "Don't—"

"I'm telling you to go. Now!" Tristus snapped. Then he swooped away below.

"Tristus!"

Theo ran to the edge of the platform and looked down towards the gateway. The mists had cleared a little. Everywhere, crelp were flitting in rage and distress, thrashing their tentacles around.

"Slaughter! Slaughter!" they whined among the bodies of their kind.

Dr. Pyre was approaching the gateway. Despite his evident injuries, Tristus made an elegant landing, coming to earth between the faceless man and the gate.

Theo strained his eyes and ears to witness the encounter.

"Come on," Chloe said. But neither of them moved, transfixed by the scene far below. Tristus folded his arms and addressed Dr. Pyre in his clear, beautiful voice.

"I know the After Time is a disaster," Tristus said calmly. "But is this really all there is left . . . madness?' "

Dr. Pyre roared. "You!"

"Kill it, kill it!" screeched the crelp.

"No!" Dr. Pyre said, unleashing a ring of fire, to keep the maddened crelp at bay. Theo watched, spellbound. He knew that garghouls did not choose to speak to many humans. Tristus and Dr. Pyre must have been enemies from way back. Perhaps garghouls communicated with those they fought in battle, as well as with their close allies.

A terrible silence followed, as the two extraordinary beings faced each other. Finally, the garghoul broke the silence.

"You're dying," Tristus said. "I can help you."

For a moment, neither one moved or spoke. Then, with one swift motion, Dr. Pyre reached out and planted his glowing hand between the garghoul's curved horns.

Fwoom!

Tristus reeled backwards, smoke pluming from his head, lost in a shower of flaming stars. One word from Dr. Pyre rang out across the cavern.

"Traitor!"

The crelp slithered and bubbled around the fallen garghoul in a wild frenzy. Tristus began to struggle to his feet.

"Secure him!" Dr. Pyre cried.

Theo tried to see what was going on, but the vapors now obscured his view. For now, Dr. Pyre and his slaves had no thought for their previous captives. Chloe tugged at Theo's arm.

"Come on! Tristus has given us our chance!"

Theo gave Chloe an imploring look. "I—I can't!" Theo blurted out. "I can't just leave him!"

"He told us to go!" Chloe grabbed Theo's arm and managed to push him back towards the steps.

"Listen," Chloe cried. "A garghoul can't be killed! *We* can! Come on—we have to take this chance—it's what your friend wants!"

Theo began to back away, but his eyes were fixed on the mists below, where the struggle still went on.

Why traitor?

"There's nothing you can do!" Chloe shouted. "We have to get away—and warn the world. But we'll be back—I promise!"

She raced up the stairway. With tears in his eyes, Theo followed her.

———❖———

The proud garghoul lay stretched out before the gateway, eyes closed, his stony body smoldering. The tentacles of the crelp wove around him in an almost solid mass, until he had no hope of struggling free.

"Take him to the Furnace to be caged," Dr. Pyre said. He turned around to watch as the crelp lifted their burden.

"Wait!"

Dr. Pyre swept the chamber with a swift gaze.

"Where is my Fool?"

151

The faceless man looked at the still garghoul, as the crelp carried him towards the stairway.

"This was no coincidence," he growled. "The garghoul appears and the Fool disappears. . . ."

He began to race up the stairs, roaring at the crelp as he passed. "Of course," he cried. "Spies! Sniff them out, you dogs!"

———◆·◆·◆———

The doorway at the top of the steps was unguarded. Theo and Chloe stopped running, their lungs almost exploding with the effort of escaping out of the Crypt.

"We need to hide somewhere—anywhere, just to get him off our trail," Chloe said, looking around desperately.

Theo looked up. There was the long curved conduit he had seen before. This stone pipeline, as large as a London Underground tunnel, was poised far above their heads, supported on a huge pillar of stone.

"See that pipe up there?" Theo said. "I've seen pipes like that—but from the other side—from the top."

Now he had spotted what he was looking for. In the cave wall opposite the pillar were steps, cut into the limestone, disappearing upwards.

"Once we're up above that pipe, I think I can get us to safety!" Theo said.

Chloe grinned, her face red, her hair in disarray. She threw off her coat and abandoned it in the ash.

"Good work, Theo," she said. "The Candle Man will find a way in the dark."

Theo felt a frisson, a chill of excitement as he heard these words. With every tired muscle in his legs protesting, he led the way upwards.

Now Theo knew exactly where he was going. A lifetime of being stuck in his lonely room with nothing but obscure books and old charts for company had given him some useful skills.

His memory of the network map, and the images burnt into his mind from his perilous arrival down there just a few hours before, combined to help him picture his way out with almost shining clarity.

Up from the limestone staircase came echoes of frenetic slithering.

"Let's go!" Chloe said. "Don't look back."

Theo struggled upwards. He felt blisters rubbing his heels. His lungs were bursting too. He had done so little running in his whole life, his body hardly knew what exercise was. Through dark, slippery caverns they raced, Theo retracing his journey with the crelp. Suddenly a roar reached their ears.

"I can see them!"

Dr. Pyre's voice boomed through the darkness just as he and Chloe stumbled into the cavern he had so desperately sought. The glimmering of the luminous fungus and molds was faint, and Theo splashed crazily among pools and stalagmites as they staggered to their destination.

"Stop them, you fools!" Dr. Pyre was not far away now, getting closer every moment.

"There it is," Theo cried.

The capsule station appeared out of the gloom, its elegant silver dome like a fallen spacecraft on a barren planet. The door was open. Theo led the way inside.

"The capsule is designed for one," Theo said.

"But we're both pretty light," Chloe said, finishing his thought. "Thank goodness for all that millet and greens you eat."

Chloe stepped into the capsule and Theo jumped in after her.

"No!" came a terrible roar from Dr. Pyre. A bolt of power ripped into the silver dome as the capsule rocketed upwards.

CHAPTER 21

ON THE SURFACE

THE CAPSULE HIT THE SURFACE and Theo
and Chloe tumbled out of its door, surrounded by
billowing smoke.

We made it, Theo thought. Then, through the haze,
he saw dark figures lined around the walls of the
icehouse, many of them holding guns.

"You're under arrest!" one figure shouted. "You
have entered a forbidden area without authoriza-
tion."

Theo's head was swimming. He saw Chloe put up
her hands, moments before he passed out.

"What's he doing in *there*?"

Theo awoke and found himself unable to move. Chloe's voice had called him back from a deep, sweet sleep that had been far more welcome than the world he had awakened to.

He was lying in some kind of glass-walled cylinder. The purring of a ventilation system breathed air all around him. Both his head and chest were attached to wires. Through the glass he could make out a nurse in a blue dress and Chloe, all in black, standing over him.

"What are you doing to him?"

The nurse spoke calmly as Chloe peered around at the apparatus holding Theo.

"The new commissioner has told us to monitor the patient as carefully as we can."

"Theo is all right," Chloe replied stubbornly. "I was with him. He's just exhausted. But putting him in here could traumatize him." She gestured angrily at all the devices surrounding Theo. "It's just like the tube that his evil guardian used to keep him in!"

"I'll go and speak to my superior," said the nurse coolly, and she rose to depart.

"What—what happened?" With alarm, Theo recalled being surrounded by figures with guns.

"It was the police. When you vanished from

Empire Hall, they searched the grounds and uncovered the icehouse. They had the place staked out after that."

"Where am I?" Theo asked.

"Safe," said Chloe. "In the headquarters of Project Orpheus, the new police department. You were transferred here a few hours ago."

"Orpheus!" Theo exclaimed. "I—I know about that! It's a police force—set up by an ancient Greek hero—or something . . ." His voice trailed away. Theo gave Chloe a weak smile. He had only just noticed her impressive new uniform, with the small silver badge.

Chloe grinned. "You're a little confused," she said. "But that's close enough. I'm Orpheus now too—all signed up and given full security clearance. At last the police are taking the network seriously. This is their medical facility." Chloe leant on the big cylinder that was holding Theo. "I didn't know they had a Mercy Tube here." She smiled feebly.

"What are they doing, really?"

"You passed out," she explained. "I told them you couldn't be examined by conventional medicine, so I suppose they're doing their best."

"Exactly," said a friendly voice.

Theo turned his head to see a tall man appear

behind Chloe. Theo had an impression of twinkling blue eyes and a kind smile.

"Police Commissioner Vincent Gold," the man said. "Your new boss on project Orpheus." He turned to one of the nurses.

"Get him out of that contraption—right now," he said. The man loomed over the pale, exhausted Theo. In contrast to the teenager, the Commissioner was a picture of health, with his bronzed skin, light curls of golden hair, and perfectly cut pale blue suit.

"Theo needs rest now, not a mad scientists' tea party." He gestured at all the machines surrounding the teenager. Theo sat up.

"Is there any water?" he croaked.

"That's the spirit," Commissioner Gold said. "And bring him some millet and greens," he added as a nurse hurried away.

"Millet . . . ?" Theo was surprised.

"I've done my research—I know all about you." The man smiled. "Don't worry, Theobald, Project Orpheus looks after its people—and you, and Chloe here, are now all mine."

Theo thought this must be some kind of joke, so he smiled politely.

"He means we're both Orpheus agents now," Chloe explained. "He decided to offer you a special role with the police—on any terms that you like."

"Exactly," Commissioner Gold said. "So there's no getting out of that!" he added with a grin. Theo tried to smile again but felt confused.

"We have to get back down in the network," Theo said as he was helped out of the cylinder. "We've seen terrible things down there—Dr. Pyre, the crelp, massive machines . . ."

"Enough!" cried the Commissioner. "Miss Cripps has filled me in already. You, Theo, can add to the tale when you feel strong enough. I've prepared a special meeting in two hours."

"Two hours? But we have to act now—" Theo began. Suddenly he felt woozy and had to be helped into a chair.

"Patience," the Commissioner said firmly. "There is a big challenge to face—but your special skills must be used as part of a plan put together by wiser heads. There will be an attack on the network—and upon our enemy, but it will take place when the *wise head*,"—here he pointed to himself—"are ready. Now get some rest."

Commissioner Gold strode out of the room, leaving Theo in a daze.

"Where *are* we?" asked Theo. He had been given a white dressing gown, which smelled fresh and new. Chloe led him out of the medical section, into a rather dirty, dark corridor.

"Come and see the wonders unfold," she said.

At the end of the passage, Theo saw a big sign on the wall, a red circle with a dark blue strip across the middle. On the strip, in clear white letters, was the name: DOWN STREET.

"Go on," Chloe said. "Ask me what it is."

"Down Street!" Theo said brightly. "A disused London Underground station, once part of the Piccadilly line between Green Park and Hyde Park Corner."

Chloe scowled. "I forgot you were brought up to be a mine of useless information. Yes, and this abandoned station is now the Orpheus Force's center of operations—and a secret way into the network! Come and see!"

Theo gazed wide-eyed at the signs of industry all around him. The disused station was still in the process of being converted. Chloe led him into a vast, low-ceilinged room where technicians were setting up monitors, unrolling reams of cable, and unpacking machines from white boxes.

Teams of police officers, all in the same black

uniform, hurried here and there, one or two of them casting Theo a curious glance. Lights, still being hastily rigged up by technicians, flickered occasionally, giving a spooky light to the scene. Two men in orange jumpsuits wandered by, wearing helmets with lights on top, and a woman was darting around with a clipboard checking things.

"Does Inspector Finley know about this?" Theo asked. Surprised by all this new police activity, he missed the dour but familiar face of the officer he knew.

Chloe's face fell.

"Poor old Finley has been taken off the case," she sighed. "No sign of him anywhere. Commissioner Gold has taken over now. This is a whole new ball game."

They sat together on a pile of boxes, drinking water from a cooler that was still half-covered in its original wrapping. The cold water tasted delicious after the ashy depths of the network.

They watched as Orpheus officers flitted by on endless urgent errands.

"It's all coming back to me now," Theo said.

"Shame," replied Chloe. "Wish I could forget the crelp. I'll be having nightmares about them for years."

Theo looked surprised. "I didn't think anything could give *you* nightmares, Chloe."

"Are you kidding?" she replied. "Nightmares come with the Vigilance territory. Can you imagine what it was like, growing up with all this talk of evil societies and smoglodytes being whispered around me? And then not being allowed to talk about it?" Chloe gave a wan smile.

"I didn't let on to my guardians at the time, but it used to terrify me. Sometimes I just wanted it all to go away, so I could just be a normal girl and think about princesses and ponies."

"Really?" Theo looked surprised.

"No, I made that bit up," Chloe said. "I used to like terrorizing Mr. Norrowmore's cat and setting fire to things in his secret lab."

Theo smiled, then the pair lapsed into silence.

"It was strange, wasn't it?" Theo said suddenly.

Chloe looked at him, amused. "Strange?" she echoed with mock astonishment. "After all we've just been through! What part did the Candle Man find strange? Narrow it down a bit!"

"When Tristus faced Dr. Pyre, he . . ." His voice trailed away.

"I thought Tristus was going to fight him," Chloe said.

"But Tristus is an *asraghoul*." Theo stressed the word with great significance. "He's a special kind of garghoul—a kind of teacher, a guide. He said he wanted to help Dr. Pyre! But it all went wrong!"

"Why do you think Dr. Pyre called Tristus a traitor?"

Theo frowned. "Tristus told me that in the old days, he was awoken by the original Philanthropist. The bad guys expected the garghouls to work for them. But Tristus turned good and sided with the original Candle Man."

"Hence 'traitor,' I suppose," said Chloe. "Well, I think he's cool. I just hope we can get down there in time to help him like he helped us."

Theo awoke. It was half past three in the afternoon, according to the big clock on the wall of the ward. He had been resting—on doctor's orders—while Chloe went away on a round of briefings.

A nurse stood next to his bed and beside her was a man in a quaint blue uniform, with white piping along the shoulders, wearing a peaked cap.

"Lord Gold's chauffeur," the nurse whispered. "We are honored."

"Ahem." The man coughed politely. "Lord Gold

wishes you to take afternoon tea with him."

"*Lord* Gold?" Theo sounded surprised.

"Our new commissioner of police is also a member of the aristocracy," the nurse explained. "One of the richest men in the country. He's poured loads of his own resources into Orpheus. Not everyone gets invited to tea, you know."

It all passed in something of a daze. Theo watched the outskirts of London roll by the car window, then was driven through what seemed like a tunnel of overarching trees, out to an enormous country estate.

Theo gazed about him in wonder. He had never seen such things before, except in his books and dreams. They drove up a long gravel drive and stopped in front of an enormous white mansion, with gleaming white columns supporting an ornate arched entrance.

Theo was taken up the steps to the front door.

"Push the bell and wait here," the chauffeur said. He went back to his warm car.

The door slowly opened, and a kind voice invited him to enter. As he crossed the threshold Theo stared in amazement. A cheerful, plump figure in a golden waistcoat and pale gray suit welcomed him in.

It was his old butler, Mr. Nicely.

CHAPTER 22

NICELY SITUATED

"JUST OUR LITTLE SURPRISE, Master Theo," Mr. Nicely said. Theo gazed at his old butler. When Theo had been a captive of Dr. Saint, Mr. Nicely had been one of the Three—the sole three people Theo was allowed to see, who ran every detail of his life and confined him to three rooms. Theo still hated the number three because of it.

Mr. Nicely had been part of the evil plan to shut Theo away from the outside world and study his special powers. But at the last moment, Mr. Nicely had helped save Theo's life. Seeing the chubby, smiling man now brought back a rush of mixed memories.

"What are you doing here?" Theo gasped. "Inspector Finley told me you were in prison awaiting trial."

Mr. Nicely made a face at the mention of Inspector Finley.

"He isn't in charge anymore." Mr. Nicely sniffed. "Thank goodness. This was His Lordship's idea. Lord Gold says he needs my expert knowledge of Dr. Saint and his doings. So he's keeping me close to hand, as it were."

Theo followed Mr. Nicely down a long hall lined with statues of great men, scientists, and philosophers. Theo had no idea what their names were, but the solemn statues seemed to somehow create a hush in the air. Just before they reached the doorway at the end, the butler turned to face Theo.

"The idea being, if it might be all right with you, that if I—ahem—help sufficiently in this business and give away enough of Dr. Saint's secrets, then Lord Gold might let me free . . . to go and work at Empire Hall again."

Theo smiled. He almost wanted to hug his old butler but didn't quite know how to go about it. They both exchanged an embarrassed look.

"Displays of affection cause envy and resentment among members of a household," Mr. Nicely said, quoting Dr. Saint.

"They are selfish and cause discomfort to sensible individuals," completed Theo. They both grinned.

They arrived in a vast, beautiful library. A central reading table was surrounded by a series of enormous globes, depicting the earth, moon, and various planetary bodies. Shelves radiated outwards in a mazelike pattern, suggesting a labyrinth of knowledge. The high ceiling, adorned with paintings of heavenly clouds and cherubs, rose into an ornate dome.

"Does this all belong to Lord Gold?" Theo was struck with awe. It seemed to him that the police chief must be more like a king than an ordinary man.

"Everything you see belongs to me," said a familiar, warm voice. Theo turned to see the Commissioner striding towards him. "Well, everything and nothing," he remarked. "I feel that knowledge, beauty, wisdom"—he gestured at the books and statues all around him—"all such things truly belong not to any one man but to the whole human race."

Theo felt too shy to speak, but deep down he agreed with the sentiments of this extraordinary man.

"Golden words, Lord Commissioner Gold," Mr. Nicely observed.

"But there is one thing more important than all

the knowledge of the world," said Lord Gold. "And that is afternoon tea. Are we ready, Mr. Nicely?"

"All in hand, sir," Mr. Nicely said as a maid appeared from a side door with a shining silver cart.

"Tea?" offered Lord Gold. "We have English Breakfast, chamomile, nettle, mint, Chinese green . . . ?"

Theo eyed the range of pots and sachets with astonishment. He settled for nettle and a fascinating pink cupcake decorated with silver sugar balls.

"You show excellent taste," Lord Gold remarked approvingly.

"It's very kind of you — Your Lordship," he said. He had been racking his brain for the correct mode of address for a Lord and a Commissioner of police, and decided to follow Mr. Nicely's example. "But I feel bad, having tea while my friends are down there in the network — slaving for Dr. Pyre, and only drinking cave water."

Lord Gold bit into a thin cracker that was lightly buttered and sprinkled with cress. He raised a finger with gentle authority.

"Theo, you and I may be enjoying some civilized refreshment, but back there at Down Street, not a moment is being wasted in assembling our forces."

Theo felt ashamed of his own impatience. Of course Lord Gold had everything in hand. And perhaps afternoon tea was more important than a young person like Theo could realize.

"And can I suggest that *this* is important," Lord Gold said, drawing an imaginary line in the air between Theo and himself with a sun-browned finger.

"You and I," he continued, "we have to know each other, trust each other, *be* each other!"

Theo almost choked on a gulp of nettle tea that threatened to go down the wrong way.

"Be each other?"

Theo frowned. The last person who had wanted to be him had been Dr. Saint. He had stolen Theo's powers with disastrous consequences.

Lord Gold smiled.

"Excuse me," he said with a grave look. "Like my heroes around me"—he gestured at the statues and portraits of great figures of the past—"I am somewhat of the philosopher." He rose and, with a faraway air, spun his enormous globe of the world.

"It is an idea I have," Lord Gold explained, "that in order to survive, the human race must rise above mere individuality. People must forget what *they* want and act for the good of all. My aims become yours and yours mine. We become each other, and in doing so we achieve things that mere individuals cannot."

Theo sipped his tea and nodded his head in agreement. Being with such a learned man made him wish to appear clever himself.

"Are you ready," Lord Gold asked, "to forget your own worries and think as I think? Believe as I believe?"

"Yes, sir," Theo said quietly. A sense of relief filled him. He liked being told what to do. Thinking for himself had been one of the hardest parts of all his adventures, since he had escaped his old guardian.

"The fate of our dear friends—our dear city, even—is at stake," Lord Gold said. "Only I have the knowledge to handle the crisis." He looked meaningfully down at Theo. "And I am convinced that only you, Theo, have the power to defeat Dr. Pyre."

The sudden arrival of the name of his deadly enemy into the conversation made Theo almost as uneasy as if the faceless, fire-wielding figure had just come through the door.

"My friends don't seem to think I'm ready to face him yet," Theo said.

Lord Gold nodded his head, as if in agreement.

"There are legends," he said, "that suggest Dr. Pyre was the man who destroyed the original Candle Man."

Theo nodded, his spirits sinking. Lord Gold gave

a smile that revealed tiny lines crinkling all over his bronzed face.

"They are not true. I have read the old police files, in Scotland Yard's Black Museum of Crime. I've pored over the Victorian newspapers at the British Library.

"There is no evidence, in any record of the time, that the power of the Candle Man was ever defeated."

Theo looked up at his host, hardly daring to believe this good news.

"But Chloe said—"

Lord Gold laughed. He motioned for Theo to follow him towards the door. "Detective Sergeant Cripps—for I have promoted her—is now part of a great plan to turn the tables on this Dr. Pyre. I think you will find she has changed her tune. And you, of course, are part of the plan too. All will be revealed tomorrow."

Theo found himself back on the gravel outside. Night had fallen. The luxury car was purring on the drive, all set to whisk Theo back to Down Street.

"With you and Sergeant Cripps working for Orpheus," Lord Gold said, "I think we shall be just about ready for anything. Farewell—for a short while!"

Theo sank back in the soft red leather, his mind reeling. Theo's guardian, Dr. Saint, had been an imposing figure to face every day, but Lord Gold seemed to be altogether more dazzling.

Back at Down Street, he was surprised to see a grim, helmeted figure waiting for him at the ward. Then, with a strange misgiving, he realized it was Chloe.

"Promoted!" Theo said.

"A big cheese now," she said, taking off her helmet. Chloe smiled, but her eyes seemed to tell another story. She looked tired and worried.

"I'm afraid it rather changes things. Now that you're in Orpheus too, we both have to follow orders. We can't make things up as we go along anymore."

"We were good at that, weren't we?" Theo replied. He gave a tired grin, but inside, his spirits were sinking.

"Wheels are turning," Chloe went on, "and they're making you and me into little parts of a big machine. I'm first into the network, five a.m. tomorrow. It's the big attack. And oh, yes—we're being separated."

CHAPTER 23

GOLDEN WORDS

"TAKE A LOOK AT THIS!"

Freddie called out to Sam, who, rake in hand, was dragging debris out of a soot-caked furnace and dropping it into the waiting row of trucks. Although it seemed that they had been slaving in the ash tunnel for days, it was less than fifteen hours since they had last seen Theo.

Sam dropped the rake and joined Freddie. With unusual boldness, the young lord had stopped working and crept along the tunnel to the end. From here, the two captives could peer down, over a railing, towards the Furnace's main entrance. There was great excitement, as Dr. Pyre had returned from the mission to the Crypt. Sam stared, half in hope, half in fear, but saw no sign of his friends.

"No Theo! No Chloe!"

"Looks like they've flown the coop," observed Freddie. "But take a gander at this!"

Coming towards the Furnace was a horde of crelp, carrying a dark figure wrapped in many tendrils.

"Look at the head—those horns," gasped Freddie. "It's a garghoul."

The momentous arrival had caught the attention of most of the workforce. Crelp scurried past to gather news. Even Hollister had stopped bullying the slaves to take a look.

"Right," said Sam. "Here's my chance!"

"What?"

"While everyone's distracted. I'm going down to the dungeons. I heard old Hollister say they're just underneath us. The rumor is they've got Grandad down there. I have to make sure he's all right!"

Freddie gave Sam a long look. "You're crazy," he said. "They'll kill you if they catch you. That Hollister—he's a thug. He'd love an excuse to crack your skull, believe me!"

"I didn't know you cared!" Sam said with a grin. "You'll just have to work like two men, so nobody notices."

Freddie looked so dismayed at the prospect of

working harder that Sam felt a pang of pity for him.

"Sorry, Freddie," Sam sighed, "but I've got to see Magnus. You'd go if it were your dad down there."

Freddie turned away. "You've got to be joking," he groaned, and picked up his rake. "Push off, then. But be quick!"

Sam ducked down behind the trucks again and scuttled off to the stairway. He rushed down the stone steps and was soon in the lower tunnel. Dark, airless, and hot, it made him feel sick just being there. But he put the discomfort out of his mind. All that mattered now was finding his grandad.

At the first fork in the passageway, Sam stopped and clapped his hand to his head in dismay. Already, he was in danger of getting lost. He looked around, took a deep breath, and tried not to panic.

Then, by the light of a fungus globe, he noticed something. The right-hand passage was covered with a fine layer of the soot—the ever-present mantle of dust that coated everything in the Furnace. But in the left-hand tunnel, freshly disturbed ash was brushed into little streaks by the telltale passing of crelp tentacles.

"Someone has been down here," Sam told himself. At the next corner, he spotted the clear print of a human foot.

In moments he was at the dungeon door. He pushed his face up to the narrow, barred window and saw Magnus lying down on a stone bed. Sam stared as if the old cemetery keeper were a mirage that might disappear at any moment.

"Grandad!" Sam called as loudly as he dared. "It's me!"

Magnus opened one wary eye.

"Sam?" he gasped. "Thank heaven you're all right!" The old man rose stiffly and walked to the cell door. "You have to go!" he croaked. "It's not safe here!"

Sam looked at his grandfather with exasperation. "I know it's not safe here!" he said. "This place isn't exactly Battersea Fun Fair. Theo's been here too. There's a plan to get help. I . . . I think he got away—"

Magnus interrupted. "It's more dangerous than you realize! The whole network, and the whole city above could be in the most terrible peril. Get out—*hurrrgh*." The old man bent over, gasping for breath.

"But what happened?" Sam pleaded. "Why did Dr. Pyre take you away?"

"This is old business, Sam. You could not possibly understand. A battle that goes back to the very darkest days of our Society, and I'm afraid it could be our final one."

"No," said Sam. "I don't believe it! We've got the Candle Man!"

Magnus's pale old eyes sparked with emotion. "That's enough!" he croaked. "Go! I order you to go! Try to get away. It is your duty to the Society to stay alive!"

"Calm down, Grandad!" Sam begged. "I'm not going without you!"

"But you must," Magnus pleaded, suddenly tired. Sam watched helplessly as Magnus walked slowly back to the stone ledge he used as a bed.

"Go now and save your young lives." Magnus sighed as he slumped in the corner. "Mine doesn't matter anymore. Go now or I shall call the guards myself."

Sam grimaced, hesitated, then headed back down the corridor.

"We won't leave you here," he called. "I promise!"

<hr />

"Tomorrow, this city is going to be free," proclaimed Lord Gold. He was standing on a platform at the front of a crowd of Orpheus police officers, in one of the subterranean chambers of the old Down Street underground station. He was wearing full Orpheus uniform: black leather jacket, leggings, and boots.

He looked a true leader of men, with his bright eyes, fair curls, and strong jaw.

"We will be free," he continued, calling out in a stirring voice. "Free from a menace that lurks in the catacombs under our city. Free from a foe that robs graves and abducts citizens. Free from a threat of unimaginable evil."

That's what a real hero is supposed to look like, Theo said to himself. He and Chloe had just been summoned to the gathering from the medical center. Compared to Lord Gold, Theo felt like a child, looking foolish in a baggy gray T-shirt Chloe had provided and enormous leather gloves, supplied by the police.

"That menace was a mystery to us until only yesterday," Lord Gold said. "But now we have learned its name: Dr. Pyre."

A whisper ran through the crowd. Theo felt his heart beat faster as that name was murmured around him.

"Two Orpheus agents have successfully spied on the enemies' activities and brought a full report." Here, Lord Gold glanced towards Theo and Chloe. Theo found himself ducking his head and trying to stand behind Chloe in the shadows. She gave him a dig in the ribs with her elbow.

Only the buzzing of the temporary lighting rigs broke the silence as the crowd hung on the Lord Commissioner's words.

"Dr. Pyre is a nihilist, a madman who hates the world so much he wishes to burn it away and replace it with a black, smoldering pile of ashes. Just as he has done to his own face.

"Beneath this city, kept secret for many an age, are diabolical alchemical engines, the works of an unknown time. These machines may give Dr. Pyre the power to carry out his insane dream. Time, for all of us, is running out. Tomorrow morning, we will begin our assault on this fiend. He seems formidable."

Lord Gold stopped here and looked out across the crowd. Everyone waited for him to go on.

"But . . . so are we," he said softly.

Theo had been hanging about at the back of the assembly with Chloe. He felt out of place in the imposing ranks of black-suited officers all around him. He hoped he could remain unnoticed in the crowd.

"Come forward, Theo," Lord Gold said suddenly.

Theo looked up helplessly at Chloe. She gently nudged him forward. The crowds of tall officers parted to make way for the youngster in their midst.

As Theo walked up, a murmur spread through the crowd.

Lord Gold nodded and said, "Yes, it's him." He beckoned Theo up onto the platform.

"This is Theo Wickland," he said. "Known in certain secretive circles as the Candle Man."

Total silence followed these words. Everyone stared up at Theo. In that crowd were people he knew: Chloe, Sergeant Crane, officers who had appeared at Empire Hall. But he couldn't make out any friendly faces; just a vast sea of shadowy heads and dark eyes, all fixed upon him.

"Theo has a unique ability," Lord Gold explained. "Something quite outside the experience of ordinary mortals. Let us call it a Death Touch."

The crowd seemed to draw in a collective breath. Lord Gold surprised them all with a sudden, reassuring smile.

"As Lord Commissioner, I have access to restricted files, secrets from the past, about the original Candle Man, a figure who saved London in Victorian times. Theo is the new incarnation of this power. Let me tell you this: with the Candle Man on our side, darkness will never prevail."

There were one or two spontaneous cheers. Theo saw smiles spread among the crowd. He saw hope flickering onto grim, rugged faces. Despite himself, Theo somehow began to feel taller; new belief grew in him that he could be the hero that these men needed.

"Look around at one another now," Lord Gold urged the gathered crowd. A hint of pride crept into his solemn tones. "You are my elite, chosen squad. Tomorrow you face the unknown, but, when the day is done, we will all meet again, as victors — as heroes who have made this great city safe again. Tonight we all live under a shadow — but tomorrow, we will be free!"

Theo felt his heart swell with hope as the Orpheus officers broke out into a sudden burst of applause. Rousing cheers filled the air.

This is it, thought Theo. *This is what it feels like to be a hero — fighting for what's right.*

Lord Gold put a strong arm on Theo's shoulders, and they both cheered together.

CHAPTER 24

THE HARVESTERS

AT 5:14 A.M. THE NEXT MORNING, Detective Sergeant Cripps of the Orpheus special force led a team of twenty agents into the tunnels below Down Street station.

She took them along the cracked passageways of Level One, down a disused drain to the flooded maze of Level Two, and safely through one of the old Victorian hatchways into the depths of Level Three. Rats scattered at their approach, but nothing larger—or more dangerous—was in evidence.

Already, rumblings could be felt here from deeper below.

Behind her, Sergeant Crane was consulting

the official police edition of the network map, a digital version combining ancient charts with radar scanning—to a point that made it almost completely unreadable.

Chloe did not need a map.

"So far, so good," said Crane, somehow managing to look untidy even in the new Orpheus uniform. He had already ripped a cuff on an old iron railing, and his helmet was spattered with drips from the dank ceiling. Chloe found his shabby air reassuring. Crane had been a friend to her and Theo in the past; in fact, with this new Project Orpheus he was all that was left of Scotland Yard as she knew it.

"I'm almost sorry we haven't seen a crelp yet," Crane muttered. "After the way they grabbed me and you at the graveyard, I've been dying to try out the eradicator."

With a wry grin he held up a device that resembled a cross between a sub-machine gun and an enormous flashlight. A single red eye gleamed at the end of its dark barrel, as if with a life of its own.

"It will be fried crelp tonight—if I see any of them," he remarked.

Chloe groaned. "The new lasers are pretty," she conceded, jerking Crane to one side as he almost walked straight into an overhead pipe. "But those red lights mark us out as easy targets. Tell the men to power the *rads* down."

"Can't do it, Chlo'," Crane said. "Standing orders from Lord Gold: Eradicators powered up and ready to rock at all times. The hostile subterraneans are too dangerous to play nice with."

Chloe scowled. "Oh, great. So I'm put in charge of this squad, but I can't use my brains because Goldy has done all the thinking for me already."

"Sure has," chuckled Crane. "That's why the men love him."

They reached a circular hatchway, which Crane failed to open. He had to stand back while Chloe struck its central plaque with the *tip-tap-tip* sequence that activated it.

"Remember," said Chloe, showing Crane a long thin scar running across the back of her hand, "I've had closer acquaintance with them. We would be better equipped bringing along one Candle Man."

"You know the plan," Crane replied, walking by Chloe's side and glancing nervously through the darkness. "He has to be protected and saved for the final push. We're the expendable ones."

Chloe pulled a face. "I haven't been brought up to think of myself as expendable," she said. "And I don't plan to start now."

Suddenly she held Crane back.

"Who goes there?" she called.

"Persephone!" hissed a voice from the shadows.

Chloe looked around and saw a second squad, led by Colonel Fairchild. He was one of Lord Gold's handpicked men, immaculate in his black uniform, cool and efficient. Beady, close-set eyes stared out of a rather babyish face. *Persephone* was the code word for the operation, and instantly warned Chloe's squad not to attack the new arrivals.

The new squad filed into the corridor, doubling the number of agents.

"Any word from Goldy?" Chloe asked. Any kind of radio contact was unreliable in the unusual conditions of the network, and old-fashioned word-of-mouth messages were all they could rely on.

Colonel Fairchild looked away. "We do not call our great leader 'Goldy,'" he observed humorlessly. "His Lordship has made his plans. It's up to us not to let him down."

Fairchild took the lead. "I'll take over now," he said. "According to the map we're just a few tunnels away from the Well Chamber."

The whole network was shaken by a dull thunder from below, as if the gods of the underworld were angry.

"Shouldn't I guide us?" Chloe asked, pushing forward. "I was practically born down here. The way ahead doesn't offer much cover. Why don't we remain in two teams—half go down the spiral staircase—"

"Sergeant Cripps!" Fairchild snapped. "We'll follow the planned route and you will follow my orders. Forward!"

The tunnel narrowed, forcing the ranks of the Orpheus team close together. They were approaching a wide, circular junction that linked with the main canal passage. They were making good time.

"What's that?" Chloe suddenly asked. It seemed to her she could hear a sudden hissing.

"Stop!" she called. Her squad halted. Colonel Fairchild's men ignored her.

"*Pleassse,*" came a faint whisper.

Someone up ahead came to an abrupt halt. A couple of men collided in the darkness and someone fell over.

"Please to stay still," a thin voice requested.

The cold, childlike sound seemed to be heard all around them. Stumbling into Sergeant Crane, Chloe raised a hand to steady herself against the low tunnel ceiling. Then she shivered and stifled a scream. The ceiling was moving.

"Please staying still," came the voice again. "So we can destroying of you."

———◆◆◆◆———

"I'm ready to go," Theo said.

He was standing at the dark, grimy door of an old London Underground maintenance lift in the depths of Down Street headquarters. Years of filth had been scratched away from the center of the door and a silver Orpheus squad emblem stuck there. He looked back at his team, hoping to spot a familiar face—but they were all strangers, grim-faced, their eyes hidden behind shiny visors.

Of all the strange adventures he had faced since escaping from his evil guardian, this felt the loneliest. As the lift door closed, his heart sank.

"Where's Lord Gold?" Theo asked one of the men. "Can I see him?"

"That is not possible," the man grunted. Theo looked up at the tall, helmeted figure.

"Where is he?" Theo asked.

"He is with us in spirit," the man said.

Theo sighed. Of course he couldn't expect someone like the Lord Commissioner to be part of the mission. Lord Gold would be watching over the whole plan from his command center in

Down Street. Still, Theo felt strangely abandoned.

The lift door opened, and Theo was led out by the tall, silent men. They marched off down the passage, six in front of Theo, six behind. He felt a bit like a prisoner. The men halted at the end of the next passage. The leading officer looked around, as if lost.

"That's the way to the Well Chamber—" Theo began, pointing ahead. He had studied these passages many times on his map. "Level Three, Tunnel Twenty. We're close to Junction Sixteen, by the old fungus houses—where they used to grow luminous mold for the fungus globes."

The men ignored him. "They aren't here," one said.

"This is not going according to schedule," another commented.

"What's going on?" Theo asked. One of the men looked down at him.

"We were to link up with Team One at this junction. There's no sign of them. It might mean they've pressed forward without us."

It might mean. Theo noticed the uncertainty. *"Might" means "might not,"* Theo said to himself, remembering one of Mr. Nicely's little sayings.

What else might have happened? He was beginning to learn that when people spoke to one another, they tended to leave the most important bit out.

"Is Team One Chloe's team?" Theo asked anxiously. "I mean, Sergeant Cripps."

One of the men nodded.

"Something isn't right," he stated simply.

Suddenly footsteps were heard clattering down the passage ahead. The guards formed ranks around Theo, so he could hardly see a thing.

"What is it? What's going on?"

A ragged, bleeding figure crashed into the guards and fell back to the ground.

"Get out!" he gasped. "Get out—save yourselves! They've killed everyone! Everyone!"

The guards bent down to take a closer look at the desperate, wounded man.

"Colonel—Colonel Fairchild?" someone asked uncertainly.

The ragged Fairchild lurched to his feet.

"Do as I say, you fools! They're up—up above us!"

An eerie breathing sound had followed Fairchild down the corridor. The men stared upwards but saw only blackness.

"It's too late!" Fairchild cried, stumbling into Theo and knocking him over. "When—when you look up, it's already too late!"

Then it happened. From the ceiling they fell, great blots of slime, wrapping stinging tentacles around the heads of the Orpheus squad. One man fired his eradicator laser only to rip one of his own comrades in two.

"We can't blast them!" screamed one of the men. "They're all over us—they . . ." His voice was drowned out as slime filled his mouth and tendrils gripped his throat.

"Harvessst," hissed a thin, eerie voice.

Theo looked up from the floor where he had fallen. Everywhere, Orpheus men were screaming, covered in the soft, clinging bodies of the crelp.

"We will harvesting you now," the thin voice said. "Please to stand still and not killing us back."

Theo stared at the horrific onslaught, preoccupied with one thought.

What do they mean, harvest?

CHAPTER 25

CRIMES

"I DON'T LIKE IT," said Freddie suspiciously. "Where have they all gone?"

Sam scoured the length of the ash tunnel, peering into the dark corners for the sight of a crelp tentacle.

"I don't know," Sam answered.

The harsh tolling of a bell reverberated deafeningly around them.

Freddie looked scared. His face went pale under its speckling of ash, and he clutched tightly on to his rake. "What's Dr. Pyre up to now?" he groaned.

"I don't care about him!" Sam said. "I just wish I knew where Theo was."

"Shut it!" came a nasty hiss from behind them.

"I'll do the talking now!" Queasley, the one-eyed Sewer Rat appeared, a nasty smile on his lips.

"Here's the good news," he said slyly. "Our little friends the crelp have had to go."

Sam knew the Sewer Rats too well to get his hopes up. "Where?" he asked.

"To defend the Wonderful Machines," Queasley said, his broken teeth showing in an unpleasant smile. "Seems there's a lot of you Surfacers trying to get down here. Police and that. So we've gotter set the guard dogs on them."

Surfacers! Sam and Freddie looked at each other. That had to mean that help was on its way.

"So here's the bad news," Hollister growled, looming up behind them. "We haven't got our little pets to guard you surface scum now, so, step this way . . ."

Queasley pointed along the passage, and Hollister gave Sam a nasty shove. They were led down to the dungeon level that Sam had so recently visited.

Sam's heart beat quickly. For a moment he expected to be locked away with his grandfather, but at the fork in the passages below, Hollister turned right instead of left, and threw open the door to a cell there.

Behind them, Sam could hear other slaves being herded along behind them.

Freddie looked terrified.

"Locked up?" he cried. "You—you haven't thought it through! I mean, come on, old chum . . . who's going to work the levers? Scrape out the ash and all that? I was getting pretty good at that. Better than Sam anyway! Evil machines don't run themselves, you know."

Hollister gave a cruel laugh. "Dincha hear the bell? That phase is over. The steam power was only needed to open up the vault and reveal them Wunnerful Machines. But the next stage ain't about steam power. It's alchemistry," he said, sounding out the word with relish.

"Now you lot is expendable," he rumbled on. "And we don't want you runnin' free in case we has a rebellion on our hands. Plus, if them crelp ever comes back—well, they might be nice and hungry." He licked his lips in a horrible way.

"Look," Sam said, turning to face Queasley. "If you have to lock me up, put me in a dungeon with Magnus—you know, the old man. He's my grandad. I want to be able to look after him. You blokes are a gang, a—a sort of family. You must know how I feel . . . having my grandad down there on his own—in this awful place!"

Hollister approached Sam with what appeared to

be a look of pity. Then he let out a raucous laugh and hurled Sam, with a sickening thud, against the back wall of the cell.

"No chance, mate. The old 'uns in solit'ry. He knows some big secret or something. No visitors allowed. Now shut up. Yer lucky we don't put you down in the vault with the gargoyle. He's got a special cage too."

"But listen," Freddie tried again as Queasley locked them both in the cell. "You chaps aren't daft. Dr. Pyre is going to do something awful, I know it. They say he wants to burn the city down. Why are you helping him? I mean, what's in it for you?"

Hollister and Queasley exchanged a surly look.

"Surfacers!" growled Hollister. "They think the world was made for them."

Queasley cleared his throat in a horrible way and spat at the foot of the cell. "We're Sewer Rats, aren't we? Orphans, misfits, nobodies—we ain't wanted in that 'appy world up above. Well, when Dr. Pyre's had his fun, it's not going to be so pretty up there. The Sewer Rats will know how to survive, though. When he's had his little bonfire, we'll be kings of the ashes."

"B-But—" Freddie stammered.

"Don't leave us here!" shouted Sam. But the Sewer Rats were gone.

"What, by all the moons, are you doing?" Tristus snarled.

Dr. Pyre stood before him, a golden cage separating him from the garghoul. They were far below the level of the dungeons, deep down among the silver wheels and spires of the Wonderful Machines. The garghoul was clutching at the bars angrily.

"You will never escape from there, treacherous one!" Dr. Pyre gloated. "Those bars are made from Oronium, the alchemist's own metal. A stone prison could not hold you, I know that well—garghouls can speak to stone—but Oronium will hold you forever."

Tristus still tested the bars.

"I know you, Dr. Pyre," he said grimly. "I know your secret."

Dr. Pyre turned away from his prisoner. "The secrets are all gone now," he said. "They have no power. Only actions have power—and that is what I am taking."

"What are you planning?"

"Destruction," Dr. Pyre said. "The biggest catastrophe this underworld has ever seen."

Tristus looked dismayed. "I used to think your madness was just an act. Now I believe you are truly insane."

Dr. Pyre faced the garghoul, his hands flickering with fire as his rage grew.

"You dare to talk about sanity to me—do you deny my accusation . . . traitor?"

"I do deny it," Tristus replied. He smashed against the bars with a futile fist.

"If you would but listen! I could tell you many things—"

Dr. Pyre allowed himself a cold laugh. "I've listened to too many lies in my life," he said. "Now, nothing will distract me from my purpose."

"They are not lies—"

"All of the world above us is nothing more," Dr. Pyre interrupted. "Only fire can save us now. I see you are not *for* me, so I consider you against me!"

"I am against the madness," Tristus cried out as Dr. Pyre strode towards the doorway. "Not against you!"

Dr. Pyre halted for a moment at the door and looked back with his shadowed, glinting eyes.

"The madness is all that is left of me," he said.

CHAPTER 26

FRIENDS IN NEED

*T*HEY'VE KILLED THEM ALL.

Colonel Fairchild's words echoed in Theo's ears amongst the screams and cries in the tunnel.

All?

He raised a glowing hand to fend off a tentacle. Everywhere, Orpheus officers were being suffocated under the slimy bodies of the crelp that had attacked from above.

Had Chloe, too, died this way?

Thwoom! Theo reached out and exploded the creature that was trying to engulf him.

"Please to putting away horrible glow—glowing— hands, please," another crelp hissed in a polite tone as its tendrils snaked round his legs.

Theo grimaced and plunged his fingers deep into the crelp's slimy body.

Whoom!

Steaming slime streaked Theo's face as the creature perished. Theo noticed blood streaming from a gash in his arm, where a spiny tentacle had ripped into his skin. Yet he was too numb with horror to register the pain.

"Fall back to the lift shaft," Colonel Fairchild screeched out. Theo could see the wounded man, his uniform in shreds, turn and stagger away into the darkness. A couple of other officers followed.

They'll never make it, Theo thought. *Not without my help.*

"Stand still to dying—to die," requested one of the crelp. "Don't you really wanting to die?"

"No!" screamed Theo, ignoring the pain of his scratched limbs as he dived to touch the nearest crelp. It went up in a howling hiss of smoke.

He blocked the middle of the corridor, making it hard for the crelp to get round him.

Whoom! Shroom!

The crelp vanished, squealing at his touch, as he held their forces back, buying time for the fleeing Orpheus men. Gradually, Theo backed away, hoping to join the retreat to the lift shaft.

But suddenly he stopped. He could feel tendrils in his hair. He spun around and saw a horrible sight. Once more, the crelp had been using the cracks in the roof and were getting behind him in great, seething numbers.

He watched in horror as their soft, prickly bodies flopped down from the ceiling, filling the tunnel behind him. Now he was surrounded, and there were far too many to fight. He couldn't press onwards to the Well Chamber, but neither could he make it to the lift.

He gritted his teeth. There was one other way. A narrow passage to his right led away from the main tunnels, into the unknown. Only a few crelp blocked that exit. Theo held both illuminated hands before him and, ignoring the hideous wails, he raced through a rain of burning slime.

———❖———

Theo collapsed against a tunnel wall, gasping for breath. He had run until his legs would work no more. Slowly, he became convinced he had left the crelp far behind.

If only I had a light, he thought. Then, an idea struck him. He wasn't in any peril, or attempting any self-defense, but surely a Candle Man could produce a little light to see by? He concentrated on his hands and willed them to release a tiny gleam of their power.

Suddenly there it was, wavering around his fingers, a soft green glow. Using his own hand as a torch he began to inspect his surroundings.

The network is mine, Theo told himself. *I will not fear it. I am the Candle Man. I drive back the darkness*, he told himself. He sank down onto a rock with a sigh.

Scary. I'm really starting to think like a Candle Man now.

He was at a junction of three tunnels. One appeared blocked by debris—more damage from the great explosion after his battle with Dr. Saint. Another led down, he didn't know where. He took a couple of steps and saw that it was full of water.

Anything could be lurking in there, Theo thought. He sat back down and looked at his cut hand. Remembering Chloe's attempts at first aid, he pulled a strip off his already torn shirt and bound up his gashed arm.

As he sat adjusting the bandage, he heard a sound. It was coming from the half-collapsed passage to his left. Something—or someone—was coming down it. Theo extinguished the light of his hand and waited. The slightest sound was amplified by the tunnels.

There was none of that eerie hissing that often accompanied the crelp. So who—or what—was it?

It could be Chloe, Theo hoped wildly. She was clever—she was sure to have escaped the crelp somehow.

Theo heard a pained gasp and a pathetic sob. No, that was not Chloe. His heart sank. But it didn't sound like a dangerous presence either. The small, feeble movements were more like the exertions of a child. Whoever it was, was hurt.

In a moment of decision, Theo rekindled his hand and turned the corner.

"No!"

A startled black imp staggered away from the light and fell against the wall. Theo stopped in surprise. Both figures gazed at each other, wide-eyed.

It was Skun.

"Go on—get it over with!" Skun cried, covering his eyes with a spindly hand.

"Get what over with?"

"You might as well kill me now! It's all over. My tribe is slaughtered. Only I escaped. And now you have hunted me down, I suppose! What a waste—of the glorious Skun," he sobbed.

Theo forgot his own woes for a moment and felt a pang of pity for the wretched smoglodyte creature.

"I'm not hunting you, Skun," he said. "In fact, I've been hunted by the crelp. Look." He showed Skun his wounded arm.

"The crelp?" Skun echoed, fear in his little voice. "How—how did you escape?"

Theo felt unexpectedly affronted at this remark. He scowled. "Well, I am the Candle Man," he said.

"Yes," hissed the smoglodyte, "but they are so many now—and learning new tricks all the time. They can come from anywhere—and *vanish* to any-where. Not even brave smogs stand a chance!"

"They can be destroyed," said Theo.

Skun crept closer to Theo and looked up at him with his small inquisitive eyes.

"You survived—for now—like me," Skun said. "But soon we will be dead. The crelp are every-where. They have begun their outvasion."

Theo frowned. "Outvasion?"

"They have emerged from the dark places beneath the earth—and now they want to come out—out into the big world on the surface. I spied on them before I—before we the Ilk tribe—were discovered."

Theo sat down on a fallen beam. In the middle of all this peril he and Skun had found a moment of calm. They were both lone survivors, lost underground—both hunted by the same foe.

"What did you learn?"

"That you are a bad man!" Skun cried. "A bad, selfish, crazy man! I told you we must unite against the crelp—told you before! But you didn't want to."

Theo felt uncomfortable. That was true.

"But you were my enemy before, Skun. I didn't have any reason to help you."

"Well, you do now," Skun snapped. "But, of course, it's too late! I heard the crelp speak to some humans they had captured. They are sucking in human brains and learning all about you. The more they learn, the more they want your precious world up there."

A whisper of movement, amplified by the tunnels around them, made them both start.

"Unbogoglia," Skun whispered. "They are coming!"

Theo stood up, dimming his hands to the faintest of glows. "Let's go," he said.

"Me?" Skun gasped. "You're asking me?"

"Yes! We could work together. Smogs know things."

"Work together? Me with the great Theo—the dreaded Candle Hand?" Skun almost bounced with excitement.

"If you wish," Theo replied. "And if you'll try and be quiet!" He was worried that the crelp would hear their every word in the strange acoustics of the tunnels.

"But," Skun said, "there is nowhere to go! The crelp are everywhere. There is no way up and no way down!"

Theo waved his hand to the left and right, studying the three-way junction again.

"There might be a way," Theo replied. His eyes burned as ideas raced through his head. He had finally worked out exactly which part of the network he was in. He had traveled this way with Chloe, once before—fleeing from a very formidable character. With his singular memory for detail, Theo could retrace the route they had taken then. It was the only solution.

"This way," Theo said, striding off down the third tunnel. "There's another way to the surface, away from this section of the network."

Skun followed warily. "Is it safe?"

"Not very." Theo took a deep breath. "We will pay a visit to the Dodo."

LAIRS

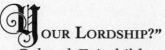OUR LORDSHIP?"

Colonel Fairchild stepped into the gloomy office of Lord Gold. A fresh uniform concealed the colonel's scarred and bandaged body, but a single slash was clearly visible across the bridge of his nose, and a shadow of fear touched his once-arrogant eyes. He found his leader studying the great network map by a single desk lamp.

"Yes?"

"You have studied my report, sir? They made me go to the medical center before I could see you in person."

"I've read the report," Lord Gold replied. He

seemed strangely distracted, as if lost in thoughts too deep to share.

"I lost all contact with Detective Sergeant Cripps. Only one man made it back with me. We had no choice but to leave young Wickland behind."

His own words made him shudder. It was a confession of utter failure. There was a silence. Lord Gold nodded.

"The Candle Man is not afraid of the dark, Fairchild. Left down there, or otherwise, he fights for me—for us. Have no doubt about that."

Fairchild's face was white.

"They took us by surprise, sir. Smothered us. We couldn't use the eradicators for fear of blasting one another."

Lord Gold turned from his map to face the colonel. "Is the second wave ready?" he asked without emotion.

"Ready to go, sir," Fairchild replied. "Are you sending them—I mean, us—straight back down there?" His voice quivered with the faintest trace of emotion.

Lord Gold ran his eye over the report on his desk. "I'm sending no one," he said. "You are free to do as you please."

"Sir?"

"Proceed, Colonel, as you think best. You are my second-in-command and have my complete confidence. You are free to do precisely what I want you to do."

"Yes, sir," Fairchild replied, a little puzzled.

Lord Gold rose and walked with Colonel Fairchild to the door.

"Ask yourself this," he said. "What would Lord Gold do?"

Fairchild nodded, a little blood returning to his babylike face. "Yes, sir. You would want me to lead the reinforcements, now that the enemy have shown their strength, and revealed their tactics."

"Excellent." Lord Gold smiled. "Then all is going according to plan. I don't know why you felt compelled to interrupt my meditations." He gave a patient smile. "They are most important, you know."

Colonel Fairchild saluted and made to leave, but Lord Gold held him with a steady gaze.

"Do not fear, Colonel. Victory will be ours," he said. "I am certain of it."

Fairchild looked troubled for a moment. "Should I send a squad to search for young Wickland?"

Lord Gold eyed the colonel with amusement. "You think he must be dead, don't you?" he asked. "But I believe otherwise. I've studied the old

Scotland Yard files. Young Theo is a Candle Man,"
Lord Gold said with an almost poetical air. "Not
the original Victorian hero, but of true Wickland
descent. He is the Keeper of the Flame, the bearer
of an ancient power that cannot—that *will* not—be
killed, no matter what."

"Very good, sir."

"Very good indeed." Lord Gold smiled. "Wickland
will be all right," he said slowly. "He will do precisely what I want him to do. As will you."

"Yes, sir," said Colonel Fairchild.

"Launch the second wave," Lord Gold said,
returning to the shadows of his room.

<hr />

"You are mad, bad, and crazy," grumbled Skun,
peering down the low, flooded tunnel. "Taking me to
dangerous places." There was a loud plop in the
water ahead, and the smoglodyte sprang up onto the
wall.

"Dangerous for others," Theo said, "but not for
us."

I hope, he added to himself. He didn't really have
much choice, he reflected. The crelp armies were all
around. In order to get to safety and find a way to
get help for Chloe—and for Sam and Magnus—he

had to take the only other route out of the network available.

The water was getting deeper, and it stank. Theo waded through it grimly. Skun crawled along the ceiling above him.

"This way!" Theo said. The route he and Chloe had used to escape the Dodo, after their first encounter the previous November, was coming back to him. Back then, he had seen so little of the outside world that every new tunnel, every dripping passage, had been a source of wonder to him. The many stages, junctions, bridges, and stairways of that journey were deeply impressed upon his memory.

Turning a narrow bend, both Theo and Skun jumped as a bat took flight from the roof above them and vanished, squealing, in the dark. Theo could see Skun's little heart palpitating in his transparent smoglodyte chest.

"Candle Hand!" whispered Skun, scowling. "Truly you are the terror of legend, to drag a poor smoglodyte this way!"

The smog sprang onto an iron pipe and scuttled along it as nimbly as a squirrel. "Stirring up trouble," the creature added darkly. Theo almost smiled, despite their peril. As if they weren't in the midst of trouble already.

Theo stopped. They had reached the circular hatchway he remembered. He raised his fist and struck it, *tip-tap-tip*. For a breathless moment nothing happened, but then there was a hiss of air, and the circular doorway opened inwards.

"Come on."

Bedlam broke out as they stepped through. Theo cried out as an enormous tiger bounded towards him. Shrieking filled his ears, and birds circled his head in the darkness above.

"A trap! A trap!" shrieked Skun, diving back for the door, only to be snatched in midair by the beak of a giant condor.

"Teratorn!" Skun whimpered. "Don't eat me — I'm disgusting!"

"Bring them here!" rasped a thick voice.

Theo's legs were knocked out from under him, as a powerful beast charged him from behind. Then he felt a pair of huge jaws lightly close around his middle, gripping him with surprising gentleness.

Theo stared ahead, and saw an immense human shape crouched in the center of the dimly lit chamber. There was the man Theo had come to see, a hulking, twisted figure in a shabby, pinstriped suit, antiquated cravat, and stained brown waistcoat. That familiar, grotesque head turned towards him, the great hooked beak for a nose, and cavernous eyes, ringed with scaly ripples of skin.

"The Dodo!" gasped Skun, dangling upside down from the beak of the great teratorn. "Still alive! Why are the worst rumors always the truest?"

Next to the Dodo, Theo could make out the enormous, shadowy hulk of some stricken creature. It was a mass of fur, fully five meters long, sprawled across the floor.

The Dodo suddenly arose, his nose scenting the air. "The stink of smoglodyte!" he murmured. Then he turned and stared towards Theo, as the tiger dropped the teenager to the floor. "And the smell of Wickland blood," he added.

Theo climbed to his feet.

"Sir Peregrine," Theo said brightly.

The Dodo would have appeared a diabolical figure to most people, a hideous old man, in his dark lair beneath the city, surrounded by creatures long thought to be extinct. But to Theo, this peculiar gentleman had been an ally—a friend in his battle against Dr. Saint. And he was one of the few people alive who had known the original Candle Man. Theo felt strangely at ease in the Dodo's presence, despite the foul stench that accompanied him.

"We came for your help," Theo added.

"Help indeed?" the Dodo rumbled, turning his great head this way and that to scent the new arrivals. The grotesque figure resumed his seat on an upturned crate, next to the enormous creature lying on the filthy floor.

The Dodo stroked its slow-breathing stomach with a stiff, disfigured hand, like the talon of a giant bird.

"It is too late for help," the Dodo sighed, a self-pitying note in his voice. Theo looked around the underground chamber. He knew from his previous visit that they were about three hundred feet below Sir Peregrine's medical practice, in a quiet square just off the famous Harley Street.

The first time Theo had stumbled upon the Dodo's underground zoo, it had been full of exotic creatures, stamping and shuffling in the dark. The enclosures had all been locked, and the feed and water well maintained.

Now the chamber was in disarray. Many cages were empty, their doors open, or broken off their hinges. The Dodo, once so formidable, now appeared a broken man.

"Excuse my rude welcome," the Dodo said, turning to Theo, one hand still laid upon the side of the immense, ailing creature. "We have been attacked—

and I expected your arrival to mean more of the same," the Dodo said.

"We have been attacked too," piped up Skun, wriggling free from the beak of the immense bird that had picked him up. "By you," he pointed out tartly, "and by the hideous crelp."

"Ah," reflected the Dodo, his eyes glazed over, as if he could hardly be bothered to see out of them. "So that's what they are."

"Tell us what happened," said Theo, drawing closer to the old man.

"Unknown to myself—at first," said the Dodo, "my relic rooms were being raided, by someone— by something," he said, "that was fond of taking bones."

"Yes, bones!" Theo blurted out. "That's how they start—taking dead things."

"Indeed," the Dodo remarked, frowning at Theo's interruption. "I see you are quite the expert on them already. Well, at first it was merely a curious puzzle. Then last night, my beloved zoo was raided by these crelp—this species of malevolent vermin. I did not arrive in time to prevent this horror. . . ." He gestured all around at the empty cages, the stricken beast before him.

"Giant Tree Sloth," Theo said softly. "*Woolcombe's*

Bestiary of Postdiluvian Extinctions, page one hundred and sixty-two, figure four."

"Marmaduke," the Dodo sighed heavily. "I called him Marmaduke."

Theo noticed now that the immense furry stomach had stopped rising and falling.

"You are too late to help, as ever," came a stern female voice from across the chamber.

Theo was astonished to see a beautiful woman, tall, with long dark hair, striding across the room in a long, swishing lab coat, the only bright, clean thing in this place of muck and misery.

"You may have heard of me," the woman said haughtily. "I am Lady Ursula Blessing."

"Lady Blessing!" gasped Theo. He had heard rumors and tales of this woman, and how she had disappeared during the great battle last November.

"Everyone in the Society of Good Works thinks you are dead," Theo remarked.

"I was taken prisoner by Sir Peregrine here," she said with a tight smile. "But I have since stayed on — out of choice — to look after him."

Theo frowned. Chloe had told him about Lady Blessing, and he didn't trust her one bit. She swept over to the strange group and loomed over Theo with a superior air, as if she—not the Dodo—owned the place.

"Sir Peregrine has told me that the original Candle Man was often in the habit of turning up too late to be much use to his friends. So if you and your vile little crony"—here she grimaced at Skun—"cannot help, then perhaps you'd be good enough to clear off."

Theo did not clear off. He scowled at Skun, who had been poking the immense dead tree sloth.

"Who says we can't help?" Theo said, an idea beginning to come together in his mind. "We can stop this from happening again. We know what's going on. We know the enemy and how to stop them."

The Dodo turned his enormous head to study Theo, the slightest spark in his sickly eyes. Skun nodded his head excitedly and began springing from foot to foot. Theo remembered Skun's proposal of a couple of days before and spoke with sudden conviction.

"We're here to suggest an alliance!"

CHAPTER 28

THE SOCIETY OF DREAD

"THE SMOGLODYTE DELEGATION is ready to begin talks," announced Skun grandly. They had withdrawn to the Silurian Room: the Dodo's secret meeting chamber. A table made from a section of fossilized redwood tree dominated the room, and colorful geological maps decorated the walls.

Skun was happy, because the Dodo had placed a foul-smelling pot of toxic smoke in front of him.

"That's better," Skun sighed. "The clean air up here in the human world was killing me."

"Anyone else with any special requirements?" Lady Blessing asked sourly. Theo shook his head. He was anxious to proceed.

216

"We mustn't waste any time in helping Chloe — and all the others."

"No time is being wasted, I promise," the Dodo replied. "Since your arrival restored hope to my heart, I have sent out my spies — Hairless Transylvanian bats mostly, to scour the tunnels and glean information about crelp movements. In a sense, we are on the attack already."

The Dodo leant forward to study Theo's face. He raised his eyebrows, affecting surprise. "Not much of an improvement," he sighed. "You are still the unhealthy specimen you were when I examined you last year in my other persona as Dr. Peregrine Arbogast. Have you been getting regular exercise, fresh air, climbing trees, and such like?"

"No," said Theo. "After my battle with Dr. Saint, the police doctors made me spend a month in bed. Pretty much the whole of December, in fact."

The Dodo nodded. "Never mind. You are the Candle Man. Life burns bright in you. One day," the Dodo added, "you will master your gifts and assume the full power and mystery of the Candle Man. On that day, you must remember your promise to free me from the hideous immortality I suffer — and allow me to live out my remaining term of mortal life."

217

Theo nodded. He didn't really understand the Dodo, but he knew that the peculiar man demanded and deserved great respect.

"I'll do my best, sir."

"I have realized," the Dodo said, "that this world is not made for everybody. Some are allowed to enjoy it—nature's golden creations, the lion and the cockroach. For others—the simple-minded sea-cow, the ponderous panda, and yes, the dodo—we are just in the way. Clumsy obstructions to creation's great procession, just waiting for somebody—or something—to clear us out of the way and improve the world with our absence."

Lady Blessing gave Theo a tight smile.

"Cheerful old relic, isn't he?" she said. "Can we get on, now? I'm dying here." She edged her seat as far away from Skun and his smoke as possible.

"An alliance, then," the Dodo rumbled, looking from Theo to Skun. Skun did not know how to sit on a chair and was now perched awkwardly on its back.

"This morning I was defeated, desolate," the Dodo said. "Attacked by marauding creatures from the earth's depths. They vanished into the darkness as swiftly as they came, cruel, numberless, impossible to defeat—or so I imagined." He looked hard at Theo.

"They are not numberless . . . yet," Theo said. He went on to tell them of his adventures, from arriving in the network to going down into the Crypt with Dr. Pyre.

At the mention of the faceless man, the Dodo frowned deeply, his talonlike hands twitching, as if out of control.

"You know him?" asked Theo.

The Dodo leant heavily on the table, his breath shuddering. "Of course. We were born in the same age. So the Incinerated Man has survived the march of time too. To what ill fate, one wonders."

"Dr. Pyre is controlling the crelp," Theo summed up. "He's the one who lets them out. If he can be stopped, then so can the crelp."

The Dodo folded his stiff hands together and peered over them, deep in thought. "You bring me hope," he said, his words muffled by his ungainly, oversize tongue. "A dark, difficult hope, but a true hope nonetheless."

One of the white-coated workers placed an ornate water jug, decorated with a carving of a heron, in the center of the table, along with four enormous crystal goblets.

"Refreshment?" Lady Blessing asked, waving a pale hand at a stray cloud of smoke from Skun's corner. "If we cannot be sane, then at least we can be civilized."

"Is there any cake?" Theo asked.

"No," said Lady Blessing. "Well, only seedcake, maize cake, and acorn cake for the animals."

"Send round to the shop for fairy cakes," the Dodo said. "Get about thirty."

"We need a name," said Skun, his face screwed up in fierce thought. "A name to resound throughout legend, for our great alliance."

"Before I ally with you, you smoglodyte scum," the Dodo said haughtily, "what can you bring to this table? Apart from the predictable bad manners and ghastly odors?"

Skun rose proudly, standing on the chair. "My tribal leader was killed by Dr. Saint," he said. "Now, as chief tracker, my people listen to me."

"I thought you said they were all slaughtered," said Theo.

"I exaggerated," Skun replied. "Smoglodytes never tell the truth unless absolutely unavoidable. To defeat the evil crelp and the abominable fiend Dr. Pyre, I will assemble a tribe of survivors. They will be the best warriors and spies. And there are stray groups of smogs that may join us—tunnel travelers and cavern gypsies. I will sound the ancient battle cry—if I can remember it—and unite them against our foes."

"And I will speak for the Society of Unrelenting Vigilance," Theo said. "We will use all our strength to stop Dr. Pyre. That includes all the power of the Candle Man, a power that until recently, I—I have been loath to use."

The Dodo nodded solemnly.

"About time too," said Skun. Then he punched the air in delight. "Yes!" he cheered.

The Dodo ignored this outburst. "I shall also promise all my strength," he said, "to avenge the slaughter in my underground cages. To take back the"—he choked on a sob—"the dear bones that were stolen!"

"And we have to tell Lord Gold," said Theo. "He's in charge of the police . . . a great man. He can help us too."

The Dodo turned to Theo, that enormous head, with the gnarled, beaklike nose looming over the pale teenager.

"No," the Dodo said quietly. "I will not ally with the law. It is—in my experience—never to be trusted."

"I agree," squeaked Skun. "Laws are always against the smoglodytes—no matter who makes them, from garghouls to mortals. So, no police, please!"

Theo didn't know what to say. He needed help, quickly, special help to fight a terrible foe and save his friends. What use had the police been so far? Even Lord Gold's new Orpheus force had been helpless against the crelp.

"Two-one," said Skun, smiling at Theo. "That means you lose."

Theo looked through the drifting smoke at the silent, formidable old Dodo, and the spindly, mischievous smoglodyte. In a strange way he felt more at home here, in this outlandish company, than he did in the world above.

People like this can help me—in the dark, against unknown terrors, Theo thought. *Crazy people like the Dodo and Skun. No one else can.*

This is why the world needs a Candle Man, I suppose, Theo pondered to himself. *To do things that the law can't do. To go where the police would fail. To make alliances with the strange and wonderful beings that most humans have no idea exist.*

"All right," said Theo. "If that's what you want. I'm in."

The Dodo thrust a clawed hand out into the center of the table. Skun slapped his gray palm down on top. Theo was about to do the same, but the Dodo and Skun pulled their own hands away sharply.

"In your case, Theo," the Dodo rumbled, "I think we will forgo the symbolic joining of hands."

Theo gave the faintest of smiles. "I think I've got my power more under control now," he said. "I've learned to hold it back—most of the time."

"Well, for my part," the Dodo said dubiously, "I will not be taking any chances."

"We need a name," cried Skun eagerly. "A title for this historic alliance."

"I know," said Theo. "We'll be called: the Society to Stop Dr. Pyre!"

Skun frowned. "Doesn't sound very good," he scoffed.

The Dodo agreed. "Doesn't exactly trip off the tongue," he remarked. "Then, nothing ever does trip off mine."

"What a force to be reckoned with!" Skun murmured, a gleam in his little dark eyes. "The cunning smoglodytes, the diabolical Dodo with his legions of beasts, and leading the way into battle, the deadly Candle Hand! Our name must sum up our fearsome power. Let us be called, 'the Society of Dread.'"

The Dodo assented. Theo nodded uncertainly.

He wondered what Chloe would think of him joining the Society of Dread. But just thinking of her reminded him of why he had to do this thing.

"Now let us make our plans," the Dodo said, suddenly sniffing the air with renewed energy. "And I believe the cakes have arrived."

CHAPTER 29

PARASITES

IN THE CAMBRIAN PERIOD, around five hundred million years ago, the Gondwanan Jellystar, according to the fossil record, was almost completely wiped out by a parasite, which we humans call the *Siphonaptera irritans*."

The Dodo led Theo into the depths of his base, down a dank and narrow corridor. "What it called itself, we can but speculate," he added.

"That is very interesting," said Theo, to whom the more remote and obscure the information, the more wonderful it seemed. "But don't you think that now we really should be getting on with our plan?"

"Open your mind!" the Dodo roared suddenly, turning to give Theo a most alarming look. "Do you imagine for one moment that I am not thinking about our plan? Already Skun has departed to find his scattered tribe, and we have more important work. Come with me."

The Dodo led Theo into a side chamber, built crudely out of sheets of corrugated iron. The smell here was foul. It reminded Theo of the aroma of Mr. Nicely's old medicine cabinet, only a hundred times worse.

The Dodo pulled a metal chain and a dim light came on. He attached a plastic bottle of stinking liquid to a large, antique-looking cylindrical spray gun, and then to Theo's astonishment began to pump the handle, drenching Theo in a vile, sticky brown liquid.

After losing patience with the spray gun, the Dodo unscrewed the bottle and tipped it over his own head, smearing it into his lumpy and wrinkled skin.

"Rub plenty around your eyes," he grunted.

Theo copied him.

"Now we're safe to go in," said the Dodo, striding towards a sealed iron door at the end of the passage. "They hate this stuff."

Drenched and reeking, Theo followed the Dodo into a kind of airlock door that separated his underground zoo from this more remote wing.

The Dodo opened the next door and led Theo into a long dark room, lit by fungus globes. Theo had the strange impression that the whole room was alive with movement.

"My insect house," the Dodo explained. "Some of the clever ones get out, which is why we are so delicately perfumed—the smell of my Barrier Nineteen drives them all away."

Now that Theo was in the insect house he wished he had put more of the goo on. He stared in a mixture of fascination and horror as bugs of every kind flitted in the shadows—antennae pricked up, segmented worms scurried, and immense dragonflies zipped about almost too fast to see.

"From your description, and with a check through my own research, I believe that the Gondwanan Jellystar is the nearest known creature, anatomically, to the crelp."

"Ah." Theo was beginning to understand. The Dodo headed through the first insect house and into a larger chamber beyond. "And the closest insect parasite I possess, to the natural enemy of the Jellystar, is . . ." The Dodo pulled on a metal ring

227

and lifted a huge glass case, seething with tiny fleas inside.

The Dodo smiled. At least Theo took the twisted leer on his disfigured face for a smile.

"The hungry little saurophthirus!" he said with relish. "See how they hop!" Theo shook a giant millipede off his leg.

"We have Lady Blessing to thank for the excellent crop of parasites." The Dodo dragged more and more of the seething glass cases from their racks. "She has encouraged me to keep up all my old interests, long after the real joy in such pursuits has died."

"That's good," said Theo, trying to be polite.

"Bring the fleas," grunted the Dodo, grabbing a case for himself and lumbering off.

Had the original Candle Man ever been involved in events as extraordinary as this? Theo gazed around him at the massed ranks of bizarre creatures, ready to depart the underground zoo. He recognized the Caspian tiger, which the Dodo called Rakhim, and the eager pack of Siberian wolf rats. Perched in the shadows above were the teratorn—vast condors as big as garghouls—grooming and preparing their jet-black feathers for flight.

Far behind them, lost in the darkness, were other creatures, stamping, lowing, hissing, and snorting.

"Some of the best ones are too big to go down the tunnels," Lady Blessing said. She had appeared next to Theo, attired in a complete protective suit of shimmering silver, topped with a see-through helmet. She looked like a rather fashionable astronaut. "The mastodon is very disappointed!"

Theo managed a smile. Then he frowned.

"I — I still don't know what you're doing here," he began awkwardly. "According to rumors, you went missing during Dr. Saint's attempt to close up the network. People think the Dodo killed you!"

They stepped aside as an eager horde of trogontheriums, outsized prehistoric beavers, lumbered by.

"I started out as a prisoner," Lady Blessing explained. "But things are different now." She paused to feed a dead mouse to a teratorn. "Sir Peregrine has come to appreciate my work — my help here. Now, I'm not really a captive anymore. I'm more like a . . ."

"Wife?" said Theo helpfully.

Lady Blessing glared at him. "Twit!" she spat out. "No, thank you! I was going to say 'trusted advisor.'"

"Ah." Theo felt awkward. Somehow he had put his foot in it. He decided it didn't matter that much. "But why have you stayed? Don't you want your old life back? Are you happier here, working with the animals?"

Theo gave her a hopeful look, which she ignored.

"I'm here on a mission," she chirped with a sudden playful air.

"What mission?"

Lady Blessing walked away, speaking over her shoulder.

"If you are a very clever boy, and somehow live through all this, then you might find out."

Now Theo could see the Dodo, lurching towards him with two white-coated figures in his wake.

"I wish I could meet the mastodon," said Theo. "I've seen one in a book: figure two, page one hundred, *Woolcombe's Bestiary of Postdiluvian Extinctions*."

The Dodo grunted. "Now is not the time. And remember: size does not always win the day."

The Dodo gestured towards the men who had followed him. Each was attired in a long white lab coat and goggles and was holding either end of a large metal trunk. Inside, carefully packed in foam, was a big glass globe, containing a hopping, dark mass.

"My insect bomb," the Dodo said with a proud glint in his eyes. "A bit of a long shot, but any advantage will be worth it. We shall save it for the strategic moment. The parasitic saurophthirus may enjoy making the acquaintance of the revolting crelp."

The flickering mass in the glass ball seemed to twitch and throb in anticipation.

"What about us?" asked Theo nervously. "If we use the bomb—will we be safe from them?"

"Naturally," replied the Dodo, with something approaching a horrible smile. "It's all a matter of specialization. These parasites only feed on one type of gelatinous flesh. Neither we nor the rest of my creatures will be troubled, I assure you."

Then the Dodo unleashed an ear-splitting howl, and his team of keepers headed into the network, each accompanied by a group of birds and beasts: silvery wolves, outsized rats, and shadowy teratorn.

"According to my bats, the crelp are limited in number, their forces ringing the network to defend against attack from any direction. In short, they are stretched. You, Skun, and I will each test them at the points agreed. You will need all your tripudon power, I suspect."

Theo didn't trust himself to speak. He was too excited.

"We will each take our own, separate routes, as we have planned," the Dodo continued, looking up as Lady Blessing reappeared, bearing an enormous diving costume of ancient manufacture, "and our forces will rendezvous at the appointed place."

Theo nodded. The Dodo cocked his head and gave Theo a sidelong look.

"Have you ever ridden a quagga?" he asked.

CHAPTER 30

IN COMMAND

THEO HAD FALLEN OFF his quagga long ago and was struggling to keep up with the rest of his force. The zebralike beast trotted at Theo's heels now, snorting nervously. Lady Blessing was up ahead, with several of the Dodo's keepers, trying to keep control of the army of rats, wolves, and trogontheriums that seemed eager to sniff out crelp without any human encouragement.

Already, Theo feared he was letting the Society of Dread down, in their three-pronged advance on the enemy. The Dodo had led the first squad into the subterranean waterways. A horde of phytosaurs, fierce, long-snouted ancestors of the modern crocodile, had been taken down an underground stream into the heart of the network's canal system. So far, it had been noted that the crelp avoided water as a means of getting around, and this could be a way of out-maneuvering them. If the plan worked, the Dodo would come up behind crelp lines.

Skun was out there somewhere, too, trying to round up his lost tribe and bring them to the Well Chamber by narrow ways that only the smoglodytes knew. Would he succeed? Theo was surprised to find himself already missing the jabbering of his eager companion.

As he pressed onwards in the gloom, Theo stumbled on a battered and discarded Orpheus helmet. He had reached the spot where his own group of Orpheus officers had been attacked by the crelp. For a moment he considered putting the helmet on himself, then disregarded the idea. It hadn't done its original wearer any good.

Tunnel twenty up ahead, Theo thought. The fungus houses. He had often thought of visiting this section, while studying the network map in the safety of his room at Empire Hall. Now everything was horribly different.

They were heading for the scene of the attack on

234

Chloe's squad. Would there be any traces of that dreadful defeat? Would there be any trace of Chloe? He swallowed hard and tried not to think of it.

"At last you're here!" sighed an impatient voice. Lady Blessing stood out in the gloom, her silvery network suit gleaming faintly.

Theo could now see that the force was no longer pressing forwards. They had come to a halt at a wide, vaulted junction, near to the site of the old fungus farm. Great iron tanks loomed ahead in the darkness.

But in the middle of the tunnels was a sinister, living barrier. A mass of crelp were draped horribly across the passage, their tentacles festooned together to form a living wall.

In the face of this freakish sight, the Dodo's army of beasts seemed uncertain; the rats skulked at the heels of the wolves that peered ahead warily. The trogontheriums bared their long teeth but could identify no real creature, no foe to attack.

"A living wall of monsters," Lady Blessing said with an air of disgust. "Any ideas, Candle Boy?"

Theo stepped closer. It was a sight to chill the blood. Ahead, hanging among the massed crelp tendrils, the bodies of fallen Orpheus soldiers could be glimpsed.

"They . . . They've made a wall out of themselves and . . . and . . ." Theo could not bring himself to mention the bodies suspended among the crelp mass. One of those couldn't be—mustn't be—Chloe.

"The animals can smell the death," Lady Blessing said. "They're fearful—confused. If we don't do something soon, we may have a stampede on our hands."

"A stampede?" Theo looked around at the horde of extraordinary creatures they had brought with them. When the Dodo had been around, it had never occurred to Theo that these creatures might panic and run wild. Now of course, things were different.

"Yes," said Lady Blessing. "I'm afraid that when he suggested dividing our forces, the dear old Dodo didn't anticipate this nasty little trick."

One of the keepers was whispering calming words to a great Newfoundland wolf and gently stroking its striped mane.

"We need action," the keeper commented. "The creatures are getting jumpy without the Dodo here. They need to follow someone they consider to be their pack leader."

"So what shall we do?" Theo wondered aloud. "I mean, who's in charge?"

Lady Blessing looked down at Theo as if he was stupid.

"Why—*you* are, Master Wickland," she said. "Head of the Society of Good Works. You outrank me. And you're a leader of the Society of Dread. It's time you started earning your illustrious titles."

Theo nodded, staring blankly. He tried to appear calm, but inside, a dreadful anxiety struck him. While making plans with the Dodo and Skun, he had felt strong, like a real Candle Man, like the hero they expected him to be. But now, surrounded by the fretful animals, he doubted himself.

"We could go back," Lady Blessing suggested with the air of someone on a holiday stroll. "Try to find a nicer way down." She glanced back at the horrible wall of tendrils blocking the path. "We do seem to be rather stuck."

Go back? Theo asked himself. *But this is where I hoped to find Chloe. This is where her squad was last seen.* He didn't want to go back.

"What about the insect bomb?" he asked.

"The Dodo has taken it ahead, remember." Lady Blessing sighed. "Sorry, but *we* haven't got one."

Theo strained his eyes, trying to see through the murk, past his ghastly foes, down the passage beyond the fateful junction. The fungus globes in the tunnel revealed a few sinister glimpses of their foe, but only enough to spread horror, not enough to reveal useful facts. They couldn't see to guess how thick the mass of crelp was. It was the unknown that was so frightening.

Was Chloe hanging there, somewhere in that slimy morass?

No. Theo refused to believe it. In this moment of crisis, he refused to be afraid. He would not be beaten by the darkness and the horror.

The light will win, he told himself. *I won't give in to despair.*

I am the Candle Man.

Theo stared at his hands. He raised them above his head and they burst into blinding light. Theo stepped forwards alone. Focusing, he poured light on the tunnel ahead.

The wall of crelp began to squirm in the brightness. Tentacles began to move, unweaving themselves from each other. As Theo took another step, one of the crelp detached itself from the wall and slithered swiftly backwards, to hide behind its fellows. A stir ran through the Dodo's army of creatures.

Theo continued forward, concentrating on his hands and making them shine with a steady, controlled glow. They crackled with power, an energy that the crelp could sense was dangerous to them.

More crelp began to pull themselves free of the wall of tentacles, a hiss of fear spreading through their ranks. An encouraging growl was heard from Rakhim, the Caspian tiger, behind Theo.

I'm with you, it seemed to say.

An excited chatter of grunts and howls broke out amongst the animal army. The Caspian tiger stood beside Theo now; in the absence of the Dodo, the great cat was accepting Theo as its leader. Confidence seemed to surge back through the herd of creatures.

Suddenly a screeching teratorn swooped into action and snatched up a crelp in its beak. The other crelp began to retreat, slithering back over one another to avoid Theo's approach. Rakhim pounced forwards and seized another crelp in its jaws. A nearby crelp tried to wrap its spiny tentacles around Rakhim's neck, but Theo swiftly touched the tendrils with his fingers, and the whole crelp went up in a flash of green flame.

The onslaught began. In seconds, rats, wolves, and trogontheriums were tearing into the crelp with flashing, sharp teeth. Whenever the crelp tried to fight back Theo was there, his hands a blur of lightning, filling the tunnel with stinking, burning, molten crelp slime.

"Now we're cooking!" said Lady Blessing as she followed carefully in Theo's footsteps. "It's such fun to have you on our side, Theo darling."

<hr />

The battle for Junction 16 was soon over. Terrified of Theo's power, fleeing in panic, the crelp were easy targets for the Dodo's horde. Sharp-taloned tera-torn, savage wolves, and nimble, ferocious rats soon sent them scattering, wailing, into the gloom.

Theo led the way across the junction and to the passages beyond. The bodies of Orpheus officers lay here and there, among fallen eradicator weapons and torn remains of crelp.

As Theo stared at the nightmarish scene, he noticed something even more shocking. Close up, he could see that the bodies were strangely flat, their skins spread out and grotesquely floppy. In a moment of realization, he saw what had happened to them.

Their bones had been taken.

Theo looked this way and that, a glitter of dread in his eyes. Would he see a sign, a trace of his friend?

"What are you looking for?" one of the men asked. Theo did not reply.

"We should move on," Lady Blessing urged.

But Theo did not want to move on. He was staring down the passage to his left, suddenly transfixed by an astonishing sight.

Walking towards him was a girl, glowing with a ghostly light.

CHAPTER 31

SURROUNDED

EAR AS WELL AS astonishment filled Theo's eyes as he stared at the glowing figure, who was stepping over dead crelp bodies and moving towards him.

"Chloe! You . . . You're . . . You're not dead are you?"

Chloe laughed. "That's a bit of a daft question, even for you!" she replied, grinning. Her dark hair stuck outwards in an untidy shock, and she was wearing shredded rags.

Theo still stared wide-eyed.

"But you're glowing!" he gasped. "I thought you might be a ghost."

Chloe looked at her hands and frowned. "Of course!" she exclaimed. "The fungus!"

A snort was heard from Rakhim, and the big Caspian tiger began to sniff around at the bulky metal vats that lined the walls of the passageway.

"We were ambushed by the crelp," Chloe said, turning to follow Rakhim. "There were too many of them to fight. We got cut off from Colonel Fairchild." She was no longer smiling now, her face drained and pale.

"Suddenly I remembered where we were—near these old fungus houses. I've passed them countless times in my work for the Society of Unrelenting Vigilance. This is where we grow the glow-mold that powers the fungus globes. These old iron vats made perfect hideaways that even the crelp couldn't get into."

Chloe pressed a code into a small panel at the side of an iron door.

"I managed to lock a few survivors in here before I hid myself in one of the other tanks. That's why I'm glowing. I'm covered with the spores." Theo's face cracked into a grin as he saw Sergeant Crane crawl out of the tank, along with a handful of luminous Orpheus officers.

"Might have known you'd come to rescue me, Theo," Crane said. "You're that kind of bloke." He gave them both a slap on the back. "Chlo' gets me into trouble, you get me out of it. Saves life from getting dull, I suppose!" The gangling policeman rose to his full height and tried to pat the mold off his torn uniform.

"Perhaps you'd like to explain who your friends are?" he added with an almost comical look of bemusement.

Lady Blessing had come to see what was happening, along with two white-coated keepers, several wolves, and Theo's quagga.

"Ah, well," said Theo, an anxious look creeping over his face, "I hope you won't be annoyed, but to fight Dr. Pyre I've made an alliance with the Dodo, Lady Blessing, and the entire smoglodyte race." He gave Chloe a hopeful smile. "Err . . . is that all right?"

To his surprise, Chloe nodded and strode swiftly ahead.

"Sound war strategy," she said. "My enemy's enemy is my friend. Well done, Candle Man. Now let's get on with the job, shall we?"

———◆◆◆———

"Just in time!" Chloe said. They had reached the final approach to the Well Chamber. Emerging from a tunnel, they gazed down into a cavern with a vast, barred iron gate at the far end. To the right was a deep dark pool, fed by a snaking canal.

Trapped between the gate and the waters of the canal were the Orpheus reinforcements. Theo could see Colonel Fairchild shouting orders while his men formed a ring around him. But surrounding them was a circle of crelp, waiting, watching, slowly edging closer to the trapped men.

Theo looked on with grim fascination. The Orpheus squad had another problem. They were fully armed, eradicators primed and glowing with power. But every time the men raised a laser to target the crelp, a tentacle flashed out of the gloom to snatch away the weapon.

"Stay calm!" Fairchild cried, but there was a hint of hysteria in his clipped tones.

"Please to standing still, humans," requested a polite crelp voice. "We come—coming to harvest you now."

One of the creatures lashed out with its tentacles, and a man on the rim of the squad was dragged, screaming, into the surrounding horde. Fortunately, it was too dark at the edges of the chamber to see what happened to him.

Rakhim nudged Theo forward with his muzzle and gave a deep, angry growl. The animals were eager for action.

"Can we take them?" asked Lady Blessing,

glancing towards the crelp. A small note of discomfort could be heard in her smooth tones.

"One way to find out," said Chloe, taking a step nearer and producing an eradicator from under the torn folds of her black jacket.

She stopped. From across the cavern, there was a loud hiss, and a ripple of alarm surged through the crelp. Beyond the surrounded men, something was happening at the gate to the Well Chamber. Dark shadows, like pools of ink, were slipping through the iron bars.

"Colonel!" shouted one of the Orpheus officers. "More of them!"

Fairchild went white. Even from his distant vantage point, Theo could see the terror in the nervous movements of the men.

"Black crelp?" wondered Lady Blessing, peering over towards the gate.

"Smogs," said Theo, a gleam of excitement in his eyes. "I've seen this kind of thing before."

The black squirming shapes squeezed through the gate and plopped onto the chamber floor. Then they began to rise upward, forming the shape of shadowy imps.

"Skun's done it," Theo cried. "He's assembled his smog army! Now we've got *them* surrounded!"

Rakhim could wait no longer. With a blood-curdling roar, the Caspian tiger sprang forward, followed by the wolves and trogontheriums. Theo was almost knocked over in the tide of fur and claw that hurtled past him.

"Do something." Chloe elbowed Theo. "Something to scare the crelp witless!"

Theo raised an arm and with all his willpower made a bolt of green light flare up from his hand to illuminate the great chamber.

In the flash of tripudon lightning, the crelp saw, with horrible clarity, the ferocious stampede heading their way. Bulbous eyes rose on stalks, glancing this way and that, wondering which peril to face first. Some edged towards the canal, seeking escape from the new threats.

Then it happened. The black waters of the pool began to bubble. A scaly claw scrambled for purchase on the stone edge of the pool. A fanged snout emerged from the depths.

"Phytosaurs!" shouted Theo as he raced down into the chamber. Out of the canal they came, monstrous prehistoric crocodiles, with baleful eyes and glittering scales. In their midst, a dripping human figure emerged in a vast, ungainly diving suit of antique design.

Swiftly, the extraordinary figure lifted off its bulky helmet. The Dodo had arrived. Two other divers followed him ashore, carrying a glass bomb in a big metal trunk. Theo hardly knew where to look.

Smoglodytes in gangs were dragging crelp by their own tentacles towards the crocodilian horde. Teratorn were swooping to rake their talons across gelatinous crelp eyes. Theo and Chloe arrived by the dark pool just in time to see a phytosaur bite a crelp clean in half.

Orpheus forces, too astonished to act, looked on as their seemingly deadly foe were ripped to shreds on all sides. Colonel Fairchild gazed up at the Dodo, who cut a more outlandish figure than ever, with his grotesque hook-nosed face, peering down from his antiquated diving suit.

"We're the Society of Dread," growled the Dodo. "We'll take over now."

CHAPTER 32

DESCENT

I DON'T CARE HOW extraordinary the circumstances are," said Colonel Fairchild, "I can't hand over a police operation to a Victorian villain, a tribe of mythical creatures, a teenage boy, and a glowing woman."

The crelp had been scattered, or torn to shreds by the terrible onslaught of the Society of Dread. The Dodo had produced an ancient key to get them through the great barred gate—and now they stood on a ledge at the top of the Well Chamber. They had reached the final stage of their quest.

"Don't forget, sir," Chloe said, giving the colonel a stern gaze, "Theo is Lord Gold's special operative.

He's been given a free role to act in any way he sees best. I'm guessing it's within your discretion to let him take the lead."

"Th-Thank you, Sergeant Cripps," Fairchild replied, nodding vaguely. It was clear to Theo that the colonel was rather overwhelmed by events. The Orpheus reinforcements, their smart black uniforms now splattered with crelp slime, walked side by side with the shadowy army of child-size smoglodytes, each side eyeing the other warily. Theo, Skun, the Dodo, Lady Blessing, and Chloe led the strange cavalcade. Colonel Fairchild trod alongside with an air of some mis-giving.

They gazed down into the dark, smoky pit that lay before them. This cavern had been used by alchemists for centuries past as a giant crucible to perform experiments on an unimaginable scale. Now it was a spectacular ruin. The chamber was acting like a huge chimney funneling smoke upwards from the furnace level, and dispersing it amongst the fissures and cracks in the cavern roof above.

The Dodo pointed downwards.

"At the foot of the Well Chamber there is a crater concealing a stairway, which will take us to Dr. Pyre. I can smell his vile presence already. A great battle no doubt awaits us."

They began to make their way down the ancient stairway carved into the walls of the chamber. The smoglodytes sprang from rock to rock, more nimbly than their human allies. Skun, perched on a crag, suddenly stopped and cried out.

"Look! More disgusting unbogoglia!"

He beckoned Theo to take a closer look at the cavern wall. Theo gasped. The dark surfaces were alive: thin tendrils, like little snakes, were crawling everywhere. Theo peered at the glistening, trickling shapes. Once you had spotted the things, you noticed them everywhere, slipping down the rocks, silently.

"It looks like pieces of crelp," he said wonderingly.

"A perceptive observation," said the Dodo. "We shall make a zoologist out of you yet."

The Dodo picked up one of the slimy forms to study in the palm of his hand.

"Cellular regeneration," the Dodo commented, watching the tendril writhe.

"Like cutting a worm in half," said Chloe slowly. She looked troubled.

"Exactly," the Dodo replied, tossing away the tendril. "My creatures have been destroying the crelp, ripping them apart—but in fact we've been increasing their numbers. The severed pieces regrow."

Theo frowned. "So none of the ones we killed are dead . . . ?" His voice trailed away anxiously.

"Call me an old worry-guts," Chloe remarked, scowling deeply, "but I've got a bad feeling about this. These things aren't just wriggling about — they're all heading downwards fast, like they have a purpose."

———

After a long, gloomy march accompanied by the endless rumblings of the furnaces below, they finally reached the broken plain at the foot of the chamber. Smoke hid the crater they sought, but the Dodo's front line of wolves and rats pressed unerringly towards it, followed by the loyal keepers. As they drew nearer their destination, Theo looked enviously at his companions.

There was Chloe, glowing with bioluminescence. She would probably be joking about that tomorrow. And there was Skun, bossing his tribe about and strutting along, proud to be one of the Society of Dread. He'd be boasting about that for ages after-wards.

But for Theo, a battle with Dr. Pyre had been

planned. Lord Gold insisted upon it, and Theo had to do what his new boss decided.

Didn't he?

Other people had lives. He had only a fate. It weighed heavily on his heart as he plodded forwards. Now the crater was just meters away.

"Sir!"

A sudden cry brought Theo to a halt. One of the Dodo's keepers was running back towards them through the drifting smoke.

"We—we've got trouble," the keeper said. "We've sighted the enemy, but our creatures are a bit spooked—look!"

Theo peered ahead and saw a solitary human figure standing in their way, as if forbidding them access to the crater. Theo was puzzled to see Rakhim backing away from it. The figure was stumbling towards them in a lurching, awkward manner.

As the figure drew nearer, Theo's blood ran cold.

It was a skeleton, a mockery of humanity, built out of a shattered skull and supported on a crazy framework of ill-matched bones. Theo staggered backwards, revolted by the sight.

Climbing out of the crater, more ghoulish figures emerged; ghastly, shambling wrecks of jumbled bones, some with cracked, ancient skulls, some with glistening fresh bone.

"Harvessst," hissed a thin, eerie voice.

"Stay—stay where you are!" shouted Fairchild from behind. His men raised their eradicators.

Theo gazed in astonishment mixed with dread. He knew that voice. These skeletons were just coverings for the crelp. They had been collected, rebuilt, reanimated. Glistening crelp eyes could be glimpsed through the gaping eye sockets in their skulls.

"We are like you now," the thin voice said. "Now we can taking your world."

The firing and the screaming began. Theo stared, preoccupied with one thought.

So that's why they wanted all those bones.

CHAPTER 33

THE COLLECTORS

OWN!"

Chloe pushed Theo to the ground as the Orpheus reinforcements unleashed the deadly beams from their eradicators. The lasers chipped skulls and split bones but seemed to have little effect on the crelp within. They kept coming.

"No!"

Theo looked in horror as the skeletons grappled with the Orpheus officers in hideous hand-to-hand combat. Human flesh was no match for cruel, raking, bony hands.

"Forwards!" barked the Dodo. "We must drive a way through them!"

He strode on, but his creatures did not follow.

The crater ahead was still disgorging skeletons like a nest of unthinkable horrors. And the full grisly truth was now unfolding.

The crelp were not merely armored in the human bones they had collected. Emerging now was a horde of horrific, skeletal beasts: composites, their armor made from the remains of the creatures raided out of the Dodo's own caverns.

It was a vile sight; stripped skulls and gleaming bones, assembled in an ugly jumble, swaying and stirring with a life that was not their own. Horns glistened, bony plates rippled, and claws flashed in the darkness. The globular eyes of the crelp peered from behind.

The Dodo's creatures backed away.

"My warriors can smell their dead comrades," the Dodo muttered. "The horror is too great!"

Theo could only watch as a monstrous creature with the skull of a rhinoceros, the rib cage of a giant tree sloth, and the hind leg bones of a great elk, charged into the ranks of the Orpheus reinforcements, crushing human flesh with ease. Screams filled the air.

Smoglodytes sprang by, squealing and crying in a language Theo could not understand. Through the wreaths of smoke it was hard to see if they were attacking or retreating. One smog was ripped in half by a skeleton with the skull of an elephant bird and the claws of a great cat.

The Dodo called for his insect bomb, long held in reserve. Two of the keepers heaved it into view in its great metal case. With a grunt, the Dodo hurled the bomb towards the crater.

It disappeared in the thick black smoke that choked the air. There was a hiss and cry from the massed crelp, but Theo had no clear view of what had happened. His eyes streamed with tears. He scrambled across the rocky floor, suddenly aware that he had become separated from Chloe.

"Fall back!" Colonel Fairchild was screaming as his men threatened to be overwhelmed by the army of skeletons. One of the Dodo's keepers crashed into Theo as the man tried to flee from the attack of a skeletal saber-toothed cat with bulging crelp eyes.

"The insect bomb hasn't worked!" the keeper cried. "We're finished!"

"Chloe!"

In the midst of all the panic, Theo could only think of finding his friend. Darkness and smoke confounded him. He strode forwards, raising both hands and casting the brightest glow he could muster.

Then he saw it. Nestling against a bank of ashen debris was the smooth sphere of the insect bomb, its glass case glistening in the light from his hands.

It didn't break open, Theo realized, his mouth dry, his heart pounding. *It didn't work because it didn't break open.*

Theo picked up the sphere, his hands trembling. Ahead, the bony crelp host shambled forwards.

"Please to standing still," one thin voice whispered. "Nice and still while we can killing of you."

Theo gritted his teeth. With all his might he hurled the bomb into the middle of the enemy ranks. This time it shattered. For a moment, the crelp faltered, looking with curiosity at the broken glass in their midst.

"Fall back, Wickland!" he heard Colonel Fairchild scream. "Fall back!"

But Theo didn't move. Something was happening. The crelp had stopped fighting.

Theo saw the biggest crelp monster begin to shake its great horned skull up and down. At first it appeared, almost comically, to be nodding. Then it began to wave its skull around crazily. Another creature, a skeletal man with a wolf's skull, began thrashing around on the floor.

A thin wailing sound emanated from the crelp

ranks. The leading monster stopped its frantic nodding motion and tore its own skull clear off, hurling it against the ground with a smash. The crelp within stood exposed, its glistening eye stalks wincing and blinking erratically.

"The parasites!" Theo cried. "They're infesting the crelp! It's working!"

The crelp clawed at their own limbs in a frenzy of agony and bewilderment.

Bony plates and horned skulls crashed to the ground, as their occupants wriggled free. Suddenly the enemy was exposed and vulnerable again.

Rakhim let out an ear-splitting roar. Wolves joined in a bloodthirsty howl. Teratorn screeched and trogontheriums bounced ahead, razor-sharp teeth at the ready.

"Attack!" shouted Theo. "Attack!"

GOOD-BYES

BONES LITTERED THE FLOOR of the Well Chamber; not a single crelp monster was standing. The insect bomb had done its work, and the Society of Dread had taken full advantage of it.

The Dodo held up a cracked human skull and studied the tiny flea sitting on top of it.

"My, the little saurops were hungry, weren't they?" the old man said with a twisted smile.

"But look," cried out Skun, pointing to the ground at his feet. "More unbogoglia tricks!"

The crelp, driven from their skeleton shells, torn to pieces, blasted by lasers, and melted by Theo's hands, were now just pools of green slime.

But the slime was moving.

One puddle slithered to join with another. Dark drips crawled across fallen bones to combine with others.

"Whatever they're doing," Chloe shouted, "stop them!"

But it was too late for that. The pools combined to form a large blob, which expanded and began to bubble upwards.

"Not good," wailed Skun. "Not good." He tried to stamp on a puddle of slime, but it slithered under his foot to add itself to the growing blob. The crelp were forming themselves into one giant mass, blocking the way into the crater.

"Destroy it!" gasped a haggard-faced Colonel Fairchild, waving his officers forwards. "Before it gets any bigger!" Theo covered his ears as eradicator fire tore ineffectually through the dark, treacly mass of slime that now covered the whole entrance.

"A dirty trick," complained Skun, peering upwards.

The unified mass of slime rose like a great bubble and towered above the approaching army, swelling outwards, forming colossal tentacles and sprouting stupendous, glistening eye stalks.

"It's as big as Empire Hall," Theo gasped.

The Caspian tiger let out a low, guttural growl.

Suddenly the Dodo's beasts were restless with alarm, faced with a living creature so very much larger than they.

"Remarkable," breathed the Dodo, coming to stand beside Theo. "A perfect group organism, pooling cells to one dominant DNA configuration. They can truly be as one. If I had but known this, I—"

He did not finish his sentence. In one horrifying motion, the Dodo was snatched up by a gigantic tentacle, and cast, screaming, into one of the smoking pits.

The shocking moment had happened in the blink of an eye. A cacophony of screeching and roaring broke out as the Dodo's creatures ran amok, hurling themselves in futile rage against the pulsing wall of slime.

Then followed a chilling moment of realization. The creatures that had attacked the wall of living jelly could not pull themselves away. Theo watched, horrified, as a great phytosaur found its jaws caught in the sticky body of the colossal crelp. The reptile struggled, twisted its great bulk from side to side, but to no avail. The slime began to absorb it.

"Retreat," shouted Colonel Fairchild. "Retreat to—" He was given no chance to finish his words. Another tentacle, the size of a falling oak tree, swept the

Orpheus officers aside like toy soldiers. Smoglodytes yelped, leaped, and scattered into the shadows.

Theo looked around for Chloe but could not see her. Orpheus officers were taking cover, darting through the black smoke belching from the pits all around him. All was chaos. Theo turned to run but could not move. Slime had oozed around his feet and held him firmly in place.

Theo felt the hideous jelly sucking him in. His hands were already covered in its slime before he had had a chance to summon his power. He wriggled desperately. In moments his head would be engulfed.

Theo focused. He refused to die in this way— without the chance to face his own fate and to free himself from the threat of Dr. Pyre. His friends needed him too. Everybody needed him.

Pain racked his body as the crelp slime began to crush him, sting him, attempt to break him down and absorb him.

No.

Theo dug deep, beneath the fear, the loathing, and the despair. Underneath all that, there was a spark in him—a flame of life that refused to be snuffed out.

It's not your time, he told the crelp, as if addressing it face-to-face. *This is not your world.*

To his astonishment, the crelp answered him back—its thoughts inside his head.

"You are like us now," it said in a huge yet soft voice, like the sighing of a great ocean. "There is only the crelp now—only I . . . we . . . us—but there is no Theo."

Theo twisted his neck to see Rakhim staring back at him, wide-eyed, mouth helplessly open, preserved, like a fly in amber, trapped in the swollen green body of the giant crelp. The slime was slipping over Theo's chin now. He could feel it seeping into his nostrils.

Theo closed his eyes.

Life! he called to himself, to the depths of his soul. *Give me life, not death. Give me life.*

And then he looked at the world around him, filled with awe. He was now inside the crelp, swallowed, trapped, swimming in a world of glistening green.

But he was alive—unhurt—his body completely aglow.

I've become the flame, he realized suddenly. He had surrendered himself to the tripudon energy, the power he usually held in check. Now it filled his body.

"There will be no Theo," the soft crelp voice said. "There will be no humankind, at all!"

"Why?" Theo asked, the question forming in his mind. "What do you want? Why do you serve Dr. Pyre?"

The crelp shuddered and shimmered around Theo, as if trying to find a new way to crush him. A strange feeling possessed Theo. He felt free—in a way he had never felt before in his life. He was free of his weak human body. Free of pain, free of fear. Now he was only . . . flame.

"We do not serve Dr. Pyre," the crelp replied. "We use him. We deceive—deceiving him. The human Pyre frees us from the Chasm, so that we can serve him. He thinks we are stupid crawlers in the dark—scared of the light. He uses us to guard the tunnels, keep his foes at bay. He did not—does not know we can build skeletons, make armor, rise up to walk, and claw and take the surface world for our own.

"We defend Dr. Pyre now, so he can release more of our kind. But soon we will need him no longer. With every human we absorb, we knowing—know more. Soon we will take him too, and then free all the crelp.

"Good-bye, human Theo," the crelp sighed. "You will soon be gone—and your bright world will be ours."

The crelp flexed its massive, gelatinous form to

265

squeeze Theo out of existence. But, in his state of pure tripudon energy, Theo had no body to be crushed.

Good-bye, Theo replied to the crelp. *You've made my decision for me.*

A strange pang of wonder and fear shivered through the enormous crelp as it found it could not harm the little life it had absorbed. In fact that life was growing stronger, brighter, more terrible.

From their hiding place in the cracks and crevices of the chamber floor, lurking in smoky pits and behind fallen debris, Chloe, Lady Blessing, the Orpheus officers, and frightened smoglodytes peered out.

The towering monster before them began to glow. Dazzling, emerald green light spread outwards, from a point in its center, to the fronded tip of every tentacle, to the glinting iris of every globular eye.

What's happening? Theo was lost in a mixture of wonder and bewilderment . . . losing his grip on the world, as his own mind seemed to disappear. He couldn't hang on to his own thoughts anymore.

Who am I? What am I doing?

Where has all this light come from?

Then came the explosion.

CHAPTER 35

WONDERS

WE'RE THROUGH!"

Slumped on his knees, Theo became dimly aware
that people were shouting all around him. He felt
like he had awakened from a dream. Chloe was
standing over him, a mixture of fear and relief on
her face. Black, searing slime was raining down
from above.

"I—I was happy," Theo babbled, "in a faraway
place. . . ."

"No, you weren't," Chloe said, grinning. "You
were here—destroying the crelp all at once!"

She helped him to his feet.

"All of them?"

"Don't you remember?" Chloe asked. "They

merged together—into one giant crelp, in order to beat us—but your power was too much for them."

Chloe sounded excited but there was a strange expression in her eyes.

"What's the matter?" Theo asked. Chloe seemed slightly pale under her coating of fungus dust.

"You—you haven't quite come back to—err, normal," she replied.

Theo felt a little dizzy. He looked down at his hands and saw them suddenly as shapes of pure green light. He blinked and they reverted back to normal again.

Chloe gulped. "The—the same thing keeps happening to your face," she said. "You're phasing in and out."

Theo felt a pang of fear shoot through him.

The power took me over, he thought. *It's out of control.* He tried to mask his panic. He had beaten the crelp—that was all that mattered. He looked around and saw the beasts, including the Caspian tiger, staggering back to life, shaking off globs of slime.

"Rakhim!" Theo cried out, delighted. The tiger roared back approvingly. "Where's the Dodo?" Theo asked.

Rakhim let out a low rumbling growl and nodded his enormous head towards a dark pit nearby. Black smoke and white-hot sparks flowed from the crack into which the Dodo had been hurled. Agitated creatures circled the pit wailing piteously.

"He—he's lost," Chloe said. "No one could survive down there."

Lady Blessing stood on the brink of the pit, in conference with two of the keepers. She glanced over at Chloe.

"You're probably right," she commented, her eyes lowered. "But we have to do what we can. He's still our pack leader. I'll send the salamanders down to look for what's left of him."

At that moment, Fairchild appeared, blood trickling from his brow, followed by a troop of ash-covered Orpheus survivors.

"All this," he growled, "will have been pointless if we don't stop Dr. Pyre." He was trying to sound tough but he looked shaken to the core. "We have to press on to find these—these Wonderful Machines!" He spat out the last words bitterly.

Theo watched as the Orpheus squad stepped into the crater and headed down its stone stairway. He noticed that the men gave him a wide berth, some casting him anxious glances, as his body glowed erratically.

"*We* did it," said Skun, scampering by and

beckoning his smog army to follow him. "I knew we would beat the crelp together, Theo."

"But what about the Dodo?" Theo asked.

"He's a tough old bird," Skun remarked. "We will see!"

Theo suddenly became aware that the men who had raced so eagerly ahead had all stopped. A searing glow silhouetted them as they stood in a row along a dark ridge. There was no way forward. They had reached the Furnace, only to be held back by a wall of flame.

"It seems Dr. Pyre wasn't relying on the crelp alone to protect him," Chloe groaned.

The great power of the furnaces had been harnessed to create a final line of defense. Rising from fissures in the ground, a barrier of fire over fifteen feet high blocked their way. Chloe covered her eyes against the glare.

"To come all this way," Colonel Fairchild cursed. "And now this!"

A murmur of dismay rippled through the ragged army of injured smogs and wounded Orpheus officers. The men looked to their leaders.

"Now we do need a Society of Dread," said Fairchild, turning to Theo and Chloe. There was desperation in his voice, and one of his eyes had taken to wandering slightly, unable to fix itself on anything. "My men can't get through there," he added.

A quiet voice spoke up.

"I can."

Theo stepped forwards. He had been standing nearer to the flames than everyone else, and now he strode closer, his hands outstretched.

"Theo, no!" Chloe cried out.

"I—I can't feel the fire," Theo said in a tone of wonder.

"What?" Chloe went to grab hold of Theo, but the heat from the blaze drove her back.

He reached out and held his fingers in the licking tongues of fire. "I can't feel them—well, just a slight tickle," he said. For a split second he glowed bright green, then became normal again. Chloe bit her lip, scowling anxiously into the wall of heat.

"What's happened to me?" Theo blurted out.

Chloe shook her head. "You've been flashing on and off like a dodgy lightbulb ever since you beat the giant crelp," she said. "Magnus might know about such things," she ventured, "but I don't. It looks as if the tripudon energy has taken over your body. You aren't—you aren't just flesh and blood anymore."

271

Theo nodded, his face pale yet luminous. He looked scared.

"W-Will I stay like this forever?"

"No!" Chloe said quickly.

"You don't *know*, do you?" Theo probed. For once, Chloe had no reply.

"Very well, Wickland, go ahead," said Colonel Fairchild. "I believe Lord Gold anticipated a moment such as this. You must proceed alone." The pale officer seemed strangely relieved. One or two of the men looked at Theo with awe.

Skun bobbed up and down behind Fairchild, with a lopsided grin.

"The smogs will be behind you, great Candle Hand," he said. "There might be another way through. Maybe we can squeeze through cracks in the ground like the hideous crelp," he muttered.

As the smogs slipped away, Skun glanced back at Colonel Fairchild.

"Humans useless—as usual!"

Theo gave Chloe a hopeless look. The wall of flame crackled before him.

"Well, I'm not human anymore," he said bleakly. "I'm going in."

"Theo!" Chloe cried out. But he was gone.

Theo had stepped forwards, and was now lost in

the dazzle of the firelight. He felt half afraid, yet half thrilled by a strange feeling of freedom, of release from his human worries.

Suddenly he was through. His bright green form slipped between the flames like a phantom. He had made it onto a shining metal pathway that led down into the pit containing the Wonderful Machines.

For the first time he had a clear view of the fabled machinery that Dr. Pyre had unearthed. The vault was shaped like a great bowl. A ring of dark spires guarded the outer walkway. As the metal road curled downwards it passed through many levels. Many dark cables, snaking pipes, and spidery webs of wire all converged on an enormous black dome at the bottom. Lights glimmering through slit windows suggested this was the center of operations.

Theo walked on without fear. He seemed to have passed beyond it. Any danger that lay before him now held no terror.

After all, what could be more terrible than me? he wondered.

Is this the destiny of the Candle Man? Is this what Lord Gold knew about me . . . that I would become a kind of living ghost? Is that why he thought Dr. Pyre couldn't beat me?

Theo had now passed under the dark web of wires. It was gloomier here. Energy crackled and spat around him; gleaming liquids bubbled in crystal tubes; a fine mist drifted about the iron columns and arches that supported the wheels and spires of the ancient machinery.

Suddenly amongst the gloomy vapors, a strange sight met his gaze. There, in an alcove under the rock wall, stood an elegant golden cage.

And inside the cage was a hunched figure. As he moved closer, Theo could see inside more clearly. Holding on to the bars, stooped and sullen, wings folded, was his friend Tristus.

CHAPTER 36

UNSEEN

RISTUS! YOU'RE ALL RIGHT!" Theo cried. "I knew you would be!"

Standing before his friend, Theo studied the face of the stony creature, slightly puzzled. Something seemed wrong, but he couldn't place what.

"Theo," the garghoul said without a hint of surprise. His slate-gray hands clutched the golden bars.

"Oronium," Tristus explained. "The great secret of the alchemists. Mere strength cannot break it."

Theo raised a hand to touch the gleaming metal. To his surprise it seemed to tremble—to come to life under his touch.

"Forged by alchemy in ages past," Tristus said. "I

am its prisoner, but the fire of your touch could unmake it."

Theo watched as the metal began to dissolve into the air.

"It—it's time," said Theo. "It's time to face Dr. Pyre."

"Beware, Theo," the garghoul said softly. "I do not know if you are ready yet—ready to encounter him."

"Some have said that he is too strong for me," Theo replied. "I hoped you would be different."

"I do not speak of battle," the garghoul answered. For a moment it appeared that Tristus would say more, but his face darkened with doubt.

"Come on," Theo urged. He was surprised that Tristus remained in the cage, now that it was melting away. "You can help me! We can beat Dr. Pyre together, can't we?"

The garghoul did not reply. Tristus's face seemed somehow empty, like the stone statue he sometimes pretended to be.

Theo suddenly felt anxious. "I know that he beat you before, but he—he took you by surprise then, didn't he . . . ?" Theo's voice trailed away.

"You had better seek your destiny alone, Theo," Tristus said, his voice hollow.

"What do you mean, alone?" Theo asked the garghoul. "Why won't you come with me? What's wrong?"

Tristus stood, motionless, still clutching the bars that were melting like ice all around him.

"I cannot help with this, Theo," he said softly. "For now . . . I am blind."

Blind? Theo gazed at his friend, stunned.

"The blast," Tristus explained, "from Dr. Pyre. His power went straight into my head."

Theo didn't know what to say.

"Come with me—" he began awkwardly.

"No," Tristus said. "You must go where you are needed. But please, fear nothing on my account. My war is over, perhaps. I hear the stone calling me."

Theo looked helplessly at his friend. Suddenly a terrible scream echoed from somewhere beneath them.

"Go, Theo!" Tristus urged. "Dr. Pyre is at work in the chamber below. Matters race to their end. The Candle Man is needed, as ever, on the very brink of disaster."

Theo headed downwards in the direction of the horrible cry. He had now reached the ominous command dome itself. Pale fumes hung around the arched entrance, but there was no sign of any movement.

Why aren't there any guards?

Then Theo saw him, just beyond the archway: the unmistakable form of Hollister, the nastiest of all the Sewer Rats. The enormous figure stood, an unmoving sentinel.

Hollister had not seen him. Theo drew closer and realized that Hollister would not be seeing anything ever again. The Sewer Rat was standing still because his body had been incinerated, fused into a pile of smoking ashes.

Theo raised his hand curiously to touch the figure. Before his eyes the ashen form trembled, then cascaded to the ground in an avalanche of gray dust.

Stepping over the remains, Theo entered the dome. He was in some kind of control room, but the Sewer Rats were no longer in control. Eerie, pale forms could be glimpsed, sprawled among the drifting vapors. Some, like Hollister, were pillars of smoking ashes. Others were little more than a streak of soot, stretched out in despairing attitudes.

The Sewer Rats were dead.

Why had Dr. Pyre turned against his followers?

Hearing voices from an inner chamber, Theo

went to investigate. He peered through a final doorway. Now he had reached the very center of the vault, the heart of the Wonderful Machines.

A circular inner sanctum, a hundred feet across, met Theo's gaze. Sunk into the floor of this chamber was a central well, pulsing with pale light. Standing at a barrier before this well was Dr. Pyre, facing his last remaining underling, the wretched, one-eyed Sewer Rat, Queasley.

"But my Lord!" Queasley cried. "It—it was all agreed!" The quivering Sewer Rat pointed a trembling finger down into the well of light. "We helped you rig up the alchemical bomb! We were going to strike at the world above . . . at the Surfacers!"

Dr. Pyre's cracked hands played over the surface of the control panel. He spoke with a calm detachment.

"Moments ago," the faceless man croaked, "I revealed my true purpose to you all and gave you the chance to flee. Instead, you all chose to attack me. Your fate is now sealed."

As Theo edged nearer, concealed by banks of machinery, he could see the bomb that Queasley was referring to. About twenty feet down, suspended in that shaft like a fallen star, was a shimmering ball of crystal and light.

"This was always my intention," Dr. Pyre continued in a dry whisper. "To harness the power here to create an alchemical bomb. To use the ill-named Wonderful Machines to destroy themselves, to destroy the furnaces, the fortresses, the wisdom of the alchemists. I intend to destroy all."

"That isn't what we agreed!" Queasley screeched. "You—you can't!"

A cold fire burned in the eyes of the faceless man.

"I am Dr. Pyre," he whispered. "Destruction is the one gift I have left."

He pointed a single, gnarled finger at Queasley.

"No!"

The Sewer Rat's cry was cut short as his body was engulfed in a ball of flame. For one moment, black, twisted arms seemed to rise up in defiance, then Queasley's tortured frame caved in upon itself and crumpled into white-hot dust.

Silently, Dr. Pyre turned back to his work. Then he stared, astounded.

Theo stood before him. Unnoticed, he had slipped from the shadows to within reach of his enemy.

"There will be no more destruction," Theo said quietly.

Dr. Pyre froze, as if he were seeing a ghost.

"Is it . . . can it be, my Fool?" Dr. Pyre gasped. He seemed uncertain.

Theo remembered that when he had met Dr. Pyre before, his own head had been bandaged and he had been hidden under a layer of soot. It wasn't surprising the man had trouble recognizing him.

"How did you get here?" Dr. Pyre demanded.

"I walked through the fire," Theo replied. "I may be a fool, but I am a very dangerous one."

Theo stood between Dr. Pyre and the controls.

"I can see it now," Dr. Pyre said with a strange awe in his voice. "I can see your face." The man's voice had changed somehow and was tinged, for a fleeting moment, almost with wonder.

Theo was puzzled. Why should his face matter so much to Dr. Pyre?

"It is too late," Dr. Pyre muttered. "Too late now for all of us!"

He raised a charred hand and, with a look of pain on his scarred visage, unleashed a searing blast at Theo.

The fire struck home.

Hungry flames licked at Theo's body but found nothing to burn — only pure green light. Theo gazed up at his attacker.

"It's never too late," he responded calmly.

"No!" roared Dr. Pyre. "I will not be stopped!"

He raised both blackened hands together and unleashed an even more terrible bolt of flame.

This time, Dr. Pyre's blast did not strike Theo. Instead, it cascaded around him in a curious way, curling and swirling erratically. Dr. Pyre staggered back, aghast.

The flames began to dance around their slight, human target, flaring into extravagant patterns above his head, like the lightning of a personal aurora borealis.

"What is it?" Dr. Pyre cried out, a tremor of horror in his voice. "What is happening?"

The young Candle Man reached out towards Dr. Pyre. With an agonized expression, the faceless man raised his arm desperately to keep Theo at bay.

They touched. For an instant, utter silence filled the chamber. Time seemed to stand still. Then, with a noise like the tearing of space and time itself, the aurora exploded outwards and ripped the control dome apart.

CHAPTER 37

DOOMED

"WHAT ARE YOU DOING, you unintelligible gnorn?" Skun screeched.

The leader of the smoglodytes had scrambled through the cracks in the cavern wall, to follow Theo's trail. Now he had stumbled upon the last living garghoul, standing in the middle of his melting cage.

"There is a battle going on!" the smog cried. "Glory to be won! Have you not heard of the Society of Dread?"

"I have not," Tristus replied.

"Well, we just invented it. We are a great

alliance—smashing Dr. Pyre and his rotten melch, the crelp! There are legends to be writ, lives to be lost! And you . . . an ally of the Candle Hand, you stand up here like a statue?"

Tristus let out the faintest of groans. "My sight has been taken away," he said. "But unfortunately, not my hearing—as I can still hear your infernal jabbering."

"You're blind?"

Tristus nodded.

The smoglodyte crept closer, like a timid bird, his head cocked on one side.

"And you're just going to stand there?"

"The fates have spoken," Tristus said. "Like a fool I tried to help the humans fix their cursed After Time, and this is how I have been repaid. It is a clear sign that my time for helping is over. Let the network fall down on me. Let the city become rubble. Let a thousand winters roll above. I will stay here and become one with the stone."

Whoom!

An ear-splitting explosion shook the vault. Below, the Candle Man and Dr. Pyre had just met in a terrible confrontation of ancient power—too much power for the stone around them to contain.

The rock walls shuddered. Great cracks appeared,

crazing the surfaces around them. The machinery in the vault groaned. Nearby, one of the gleaming spires toppled. Shards of stone rained down from the cavern roof high above. Behind Skun, several smogs leapt up and down in fright.

"Disaster!" one shrieked. "The whole *crabang* is going to come down on us!"

Tristus did not stir.

"Selfish monster!" Skun screamed. "How can you waste your great power when there are cowards trapped in this disaster who need your help!"

Tristus slowly raised his head.

"I have often pondered what dark destiny awaited me," he groaned. "But I never imagined being called selfish by a smoglodyte. Now I am too ashamed to return to the stone that created me."

The garghoul stood proudly, unfurled his damaged wings. "You are right, for once, nilfug," he cried. "Lead me to the wall of this vault."

"Certainly," Skun said, bouncing up on to Tristus's shoulders. "Forwards, for the Society of Dread! If you will give me the honor, Mr. Asraghoul, I, Skun, will be your eyes!"

The rock walls gave another horrible groan. Orpheus officers up above, Chloe included, felt the cavern shake. Beneath the Furnace, in cells and dungeons, slaves trembled as the world seemed about to end around them.

Tristus, guided by Skun, placed his hands against the wall of the great vault.

Stand, Tristus commanded the cavern around him with all his heart and mind. As garghouls had done in ages past, he felt his way into the stone and gave it his strength. *We will stand together.*

It was not easy. Tristus almost felt himself being torn apart as he supported the stone with all his strength and wisdom. *We will stand.*

The stone shuddered and groaned. The walls of the vault, the tunnels of the Great Furnace, the roof of the great cavern above them all seemed to creak, cry out, sigh and protest, cry and whisper, yearning for destruction or peace.

Peace, Tristus told the stone. *Choose peace.*

We will stand, he told the stone. *We are standing. We stand.*

Then suddenly there was silence.

———◈———

Dazed, Theo rose to his knees. The control dome, now a blackened wreck, was dark and silent. Theo peered down into the central well and saw the alchemical bomb in the shaft below. It no longer gleamed with power but rested, slightly askew, in shadows.

A low groan reached Theo's ears. Through the gloom he could now see Dr. Pyre, sprawled across the metal floor. Like Theo, then, the old alchemist had survived the incredible explosion that resulted from their encounter.

Theo looked at his own hand. It was solid, not glowing green anymore, just flickering with the softest of lights. He had survived unscathed. The same could not be said for Dr. Pyre. The faceless man lay on the edge of the central well, obviously hurt. His skin was no longer dull gray ash. Now it was black, scorched, yet broken up into a mass of fine cracks, which flickered with a ghostly, green light.

"And so . . ."

A cracked whisper came through the gloom. "And so . . . doom takes us all."

Of all the things Theo had been expecting Dr. Pyre to say or do, this was not one of them.

Dr. Pyre gazed around as a fine web of green energy flowed around his body, so faint it almost seemed like an afterglow.

And it was eating him away.

"So it *is* you," Dr. Pyre remarked, trying to touch the ribbons of light as they flashed around him. A spark slipped through his fingers. "Here is my proof."

"What do you mean?" Theo asked.

"I did wonder," the man gasped, "when—when I saw your face properly for the first time, Fool."

My face?

A horrible cry split the darkness as Dr. Pyre began to writhe with pain. Green flames poured from his eyes, and he slumped to the ground. He lay there, his body glowing like the last coals of a dying fire.

Theo stared, horrified. Gradually, the stricken man stirred again and rolled onto his side. At last, Theo's curiosity got the better of him.

"Why did you say," Theo asked, daring to step closer, "that I have doomed us all?"

"What is the use?" gasped Dr. Pyre. "What is the use of words, in a world where truth turns into lies and disaster?"

Theo felt afraid. Dr. Pyre pushed himself up, racked with pain, and sat against a control panel. His ashen body looked delicate now, pale and spent, as if about to fall apart.

"How can truth turn into lies?" asked Theo.

"This world can never be better now," Dr. Pyre said bitterly. "Because of you—the one person in the world who could have stopped me."

Theo gazed at the ruin of a man slumped before him. It was a terrible sight. "Help me," Theo said slowly. "Help me to understand."

Dr. Pyre sighed. "Words have always been used against me. Clever lies have beaten me and driven me mad. But for you, my Fool," he gasped, "I will attempt a little truth. A little truth before the horror that is to come."

OF MADNESS

"Once there was a hero called the Candle Man," Dr. Pyre began.

Theo's soul seemed to stir at the sound of that name. Here, in the dark and shattered control dome, deep in the heart of the now-dormant Wonderful Machines, it felt like he and Dr. Pyre were the only humans left in the world. The faceless man was torn by a fit of coughing. He breathed slowly before continuing.

"The Candle Man was pitted against a clever villain called the Philanthropist, and they fought the great battle of good versus evil above and below the streets of London."

"Yes, I know," said Theo. "A hundred years ago."

"A hundred years ago," echoed Dr. Pyre in a hollow tone. "If you say so." His deep, dark eyes stared out into the darkness with something Theo could only regard as sorrow. The faceless man coughed again, then continued.

"But the Philanthropist, a brilliant man called Erasmus Fontaine, was too clever for the poor Candle Man. The Philanthropist pretended to be good, used his money to buy important friends, and ran criminal gangs he called charities. Eventually, he rose to become important in the police.

"From that time on, whenever the Candle Man fought his foe, people thought that the Candle Man was bad—or that he was going insane. Friends turned against him. Everyone began to distrust him.

"Lord Wickland, the Candle Man, was determined to smash his foe. He tried to increase his power. In a disastrous experiment at Wickland Hall, his tripudon energy flowed out of control. It became a raging flame. Before Lord Wickland could control his power, it had scorched his body, and razed his mansion to the ground."

Theo felt a cold tingle rush along his spine.

"Now Wickland had lost everything. His battle with the Philanthropist, his friends, even his face."

Theo gazed, spellbound, at the ruin of a man before him.

"You," he breathed. "You are Lord Wickland!"

The ashen figure assented with the slightest inclination of his head.

"Yes," he sighed.

Theo staggered backwards. His mind reeled. The events of the last days flashed deliriously through his mind.

He had been sent to fight the original Candle Man.

But there was no time to consider that now. In a crumbling whisper, the man before him carried on.

"I decided to turn my disaster into an advantage. I abandoned the identity of the Candle Man. I became the villainous Dr. Pyre. As Dr. Pyre I could act as I wished—I did not need to work with the police or observe any laws that inconvenienced me. I used my new, wilder power to burn down the hidden bases of my enemy, attack those who secretly worked for him.

"The Philanthropist soon worked out who I was, but he could do nothing to stop me. Instead of defeating him by being good, I was destroying him by being terrible—by appearing more evil. It worked for me in a way I couldn't have dreamed possible."

"But what happened?" Theo asked. "How did you end up here, in my time?"

A profound sigh, or perhaps a groan of pain, came from the dark human wreck.

"A grim twist of fate," he said. "Blame it on the garghouls. While my war with the Philanthropist was at its height, the garghouls were arising. At first, some worked for my enemy, some worked for me. But soon they decided to rise up against all humans. And the devil that would lead them was that traitor, my once-friend Tristus."

"Tristus!" Theo could only listen, astonished.

"One night, I ventured into the network on a mission to stop the Philanthropist and the infernal devices he was building beneath the city. As I pursued him, we both stumbled across a great gathering of garghouls, a veritable war council of the winged demons.

"The Philanthropist and I were attacked by a cruel *ghoulish* spell. The events are confused to me now, shadowy, but a dark enchantment swept the caverns, turning both me and my enemy into shapes of lifeless stone. Our lives, hates, hopes, and folly all taken away in the wink of an eye.

"Lost to mortal sight, we slumbered a century away, petrified in darkness. Until, eight weeks ago, we returned."

The crumpled figure caught his breath. Not just

physical pain but bitter emotional turmoil seemed to be eating him away.

Just then, light dawned in Theo's mind.

"Eight weeks ago!" he blurted out. "That was when Dr. Saint performed his terrible experiment in the Well Chamber." He looked on his ancestor with eyes of sad wonder. "Dr. Saint, a modern-day alchemist, achieved Golden Time," Theo explained, "the time when miracles are possible."

Then Theo's excited face clouded over. "His—his power went wrong. I—I defeated him before he had finished his work. But the forces he unleashed must have brought you back to life."

Lord Wickland stared at Theo from deep, sorrowful eyes.

"Your words ring true," he whispered in a voice that was growing ever more faint. "Golden Time was achieved by another, deep in these tunnels. When that miraculous state occurred, we were freed. We became flesh again, but at a cost.

"The alchemy that restored us to life was flawed. It had left us both damaged. I was hurt, dying. The Philanthropist left me in the ruins of the network. He headed for the surface, saying he would rise to power again, finish his Good Works. I was left for dead.

"I knew I had not long to live. But I swore one thing—that in the time I had left I would perform a final act of destruction as Dr. Pyre.

"I had discovered that the Philanthropist had a master plan—a terrible power hidden below the network."

Theo looked up at the vast wheels above him, now shadowy and silent again.

"The Wonderful Machines!"

"Yes. I devised a plan. I knew I didn't have much time. I encountered some villains, the Sewer Rats, lurking in the tunnels. They recognized Dr. Pyre from old legends kept alive by London's underworld gangs, and I soon persuaded them to work for me.

"Then, I went down into the Crypt and freed some creatures to be my watchdogs. I knew the crelp of old, frightening, sneaking things. I planned to release just enough to flood the network and keep any enemies at bay."

"But the crelp are evil!" Theo said.

"I did not care," Lord Wickland said bitterly. "All my heroic efforts to help this city had failed, left me branded a madman, a fanatic. I was using evil to beat evil. It struck me as poetic justice. I believed the crelp would keep the police at bay. That was all I cared about."

"But if you feared the Wonderful Machines, why did you get slaves to start them up?"

Dr. Pyre gave Theo the bleakest of looks from the depths of his haunted, shadowy eyes.

"I only ever started them up, with the idea of creating enough power to blow them apart. The alchemical bomb I constructed had but one purpose: to destroy the Wonderful Machines—to course through the network annihilating every factory, pipe, well, and furnace. My last act would be to destroy the Philanthropist's life's work."

"But why," Theo asked. "Why didn't you explain what you wanted to do?"

"To who? To the police? I knew my foe would outsmart me as ever. Look at my hideous appearance! Within a short time, with his lies and influence he would have me hunted as a monster."

Theo looked across at the fallen man. Lord Wickland. This bitter, half-insane, burnt shell of a man was what his great ancestor had become. Theo felt pity for him.

"Now that I know the truth," Theo said, "perhaps we can—"

"Work together?" interrupted Lord Wickland, mockingly. "We would fail! I have fought Erasmus Fontaine for too long! He is too clever. He always wins. And besides, it is too late now, for me. . . ."

A sudden spark of green energy flashed between Lord Wickland and Theo.

"In attacking you, I have been eaten away by the tripudon power. It seems it only acknowledges one master. You are the new, I am the old."

"But there's so much I want to ask you," Theo cried.

"My time is nearly up," Lord Wickland gasped. "But there is something I say to you. Beware. *He* is out there. He has had eight weeks. That time is short to a mere human. But to one such as the Philanthropist, it is all he needs. He has had time to buy new friends, murder and bribe his way back to power. That most calculating, most cunning of evil fiends is in the world above, mark my words."

"Can I . . . Could I beat him?" Theo asked.

"You will have no chance, I fear," Lord Wickland said. "He will dazzle the world with his fake kindness, his glorious lies. You will know he is evil, but no one will believe you. You will warn the world of its peril, but no one will care. You will defy him . . . and the world will brand you a madman."

"B-But it's not like that," Theo stammered. "There is no Philanthropist now. He's just an ancient tale, like — like you."

"Fool!" snapped Lord Wickland. "He will not use that name anymore. He will appear among you as a friend, a hero, a kind man. Beware of him. Because he will be out to rule this world, bend it to his will. And he will see you as his main obstacle."

"I'll help you," Theo cried. "Together we can—"

"No, there can be no 'together.' The power must pass on."

And it seemed to Theo that Lord Wickland's voice had become stronger. It seemed that in the darkness, he sat there, fair-skinned, with a lean, handsome, tragic face.

"Lord Wickland!" Theo gasped. "You're . . . You're all right!"

The figure before Theo shimmered and appeared to be standing, but not on the ground. Theo could have sworn the man was standing over the bomb shaft, above the inner well . . . in thin air.

"Yes, I'm all right, now, my clever Fool. And I leave you to sorrow. Will you do one thing for me? Release one very stubborn old man—from the deepest of my dungeons. He will be found below the ash tunnels. Will you promise me that?"

Theo nodded. But it was strange to hear Lord Wickland sounding so sad, so final, when he stood there looking so young and bright.

"I go now," Lord Wickland said. "I go into the candlelight."

As Theo gazed, astonished, a large, black, hooded bird landed next to the ashes of Lord Wickland's skull.

CHAPTER 39

UNEARTHED

HERE," said a cool female voice. "We found you."

Theo turned to see a tall woman in a ragged silver costume, strolling into the ruined chamber. Her wild, dark hair was singed and faintly smoldering. More hooded crows swooped to follow her. Just behind her were a handful of men in torn white coats, covered in blood and ashes. A pack of grinning wolves loped beside them, some limping, their fur mired with crelp slime.

"Lady Blessing!" Theo cried.

She made a wry face. "I wanted to go home and have a shower," she remarked. "But *he* insisted we check up on you."

She nodded back to the doorway, where a bizarre procession was arriving. Slow-moving phytosaurs, the immense, waddling crocodilian monsters, were carrying a makeshift bier on their backs, a kind of bed of ropes and timber. Lying on it was the blackened, still-smoking form of the Dodo.

"I knew we would find you," whispered his cracked voice. "All humans stink to the sensitive noses of my creatures, but you, Theobald, with your knack for getting in and out of extraordinary situations, stink more than most."

"You made it," Theo said, smiling to see the old man. "You survived!"

"Just," commented Lady Blessing.

Theo peered at the scorched and ragged form of the Dodo. His skin was mostly blackened and blistered. One of his hands was like a piece of charred meat, and his left eye was bloated and pale, and reminded Theo of a poached egg.

"Surprised? You haven't been paying attention, my boy," the Dodo groaned. "Thanks to the touch of your ancestor, who transfigured my cells with his cursed power, I cannot die."

"Yes, but you'd still be cooking down in that pit if we hadn't turned up to haul you out," Lady Blessing said sharply.

The Dodo, wincing with pain, turned his head slightly to look at Theo.

"Now, young man, be so kind as to tell me . . . Dr. Pyre?"

"He—he's gone," replied Theo. And after a moment's thought he added, "He never really existed in the first place."

The Dodo's face twisted into the tiniest suggestion of a smile. "Quite the sort of answer I would expect from a curious boy like you!" he sighed.

"He said we're in great danger, from the Philanthropist," Theo added. The Dodo scowled.

"You might be in great danger," he said, "of all, each and every kind. But I am not. When you have become a Reluctant Immortal, then danger is a thrill reserved for others."

Lady Blessing raised her eyes to heaven. "Listen to him! You'd think he came out of this without a scratch," she said. "We'd better get you home, Sir Peregrine," she added in a respectful tone, "where I can look after you."

The Dodo gave a small nod.

"Come," snapped Lady Blessing. Theo followed as they headed out of the control dome.

"The men have been studying the machinery

here," Lady Blessing remarked. "The place is a wreck. The bomb cannot be activated now. It seems the threat from these Wonderful Machines is over."

Theo nodded. "But what about the greater menace? The original Philanthropist has returned. Do you think we should do something about that?" he asked anxiously.

"Looking for more adventures already?" sighed the Dodo from his bier. "Oh, what it is to be young."

Theo suddenly felt tired and unable to care anymore. Now that Dr. Pyre had gone, his words, his warnings, seemed to be fading like a dream.

"This battle is won," the Dodo said. "I only wish to return home and calm my beloved beasts—the dear phytosaurs and the delicate wolf-rats."

Theo sighed. He felt lost, tired, and confused.

Lady Blessing took him aside and pointed up a narrow side passage. "This tunnel," she said, "will take you back to your friends. Our spies"—here she glanced at a couple of tiny bats, nestling by the Dodo's enormous head—"tell us the intrepid Orpheus squad are still stuck behind a wall of fire up there."

"Then how did you get through?" Theo asked.

"Aha." Lady Blessing looked smug. "We discovered a way after rescuing the Dodo from the pit he was dumped in. There's a whole catacomb connecting the Furnace up there with the vault down here. Old service tunnels and waste chutes. A delightful place when you get to know it!" She offered Theo the shadow of a smile. "Anyway, run along, and get your party hat on—a great celebration is about to begin."

"For the Society of Dread?"

"No," groaned the Dodo. "For the police. And we cannot rub shoulders with that rabble. I rather suspect the part the Society of Dread played in this day will be erased from history."

Theo looked surprised, but he was too drained to feel any great surprise.

"Go, Master Wickland," the Dodo said quietly. "Go and enjoy as much of the glory as you can."

Theo looked bleak. "I don't think there is any glory, actually."

The Dodo nodded. "Perhaps, but you are too young to know that. Now do as I say for once. Go away and *pretend* to enjoy yourself, for heaven's sake."

It was the smoglodytes who found the way through. Theo stumbled on a band of young imps, little more than smoglings, in the catacombs that Lady Blessing had discovered.

Theo had set them to work, finding a way up through the tunnels until they located the dungeons that Lord Wickland had spoken of. The smogs had even found a way wide enough for Theo to crawl through, so he could be there, at the official rescue, in person.

The playful, young smoglings snickered and smirked at Theo's efforts as he followed the subterranean obstacle course they had pioneered for him. Here and there, the walls were cracked and the roof had fallen in, evidence of the great tripudon explosion that had rocked the whole cavern.

"Why do they make humans like that?" a smogling asked. "They can't squeeze through cracks or pour themselves down holes . . . horrible great lumbering things—how do they ever get about?"

"Shush! This is the Candle Hand. If you annoy him he'll pop you. Do you know he's killed about a hundred smogs already?"

"No!"

Theo grimaced at this banter. He recalled, not so long ago, resolving never to use his powers again to hurt anybody or anything. Now look what he had done: added another terrible chapter in the myth of the Candle Hand. He crawled on hands and knees through the ruins, coughing on the remnants of acrid smoke, pricking his hands on thorny bits of dead crelp.

"Oh, dear!" gasped a young smog with mock concern. The dead bodies of two human guards, Sewer Rats, lay outside the dungeon doors, crushed by rubble from the caved-in roof above.

"Funny, isn't it?" the smog said. "The prisoner is safe in his cell, while the guards get smashed to death outside."

"Look at the expression on this one's face!" giggled another smogling, chuckling over the crushed corpse.

"This is it," said Theo, regarding the dungeon door. A smogling stooped and took keys from the belt of one of the dead figures and gave them to Theo.

"They use these," the smog said with a small frown on its turnip-shaped face. "But I'm not sure how they work."

But Theo had already spotted that the lock was made of golden oronium. He touched it and it melted away.

"Whooo!" exclaimed the smogs appreciatively. The door creaked open and Theo peered inside. Something stirred slowly in the shadows. There was Magnus. His mottled, bald head turned and his small, squinting eyes blinked in surprise.

"Theo," he said with a strange, sad smile. "Of course."

The old man rose slowly, resting his weight on his two chipped and worn walking sticks. "There's been quite a commotion," he added. "I take it the Wonderful Machines did not destroy us all?"

Theo tried to smile but could not. Magnus gave him a searching look.

"Is he—is he gone then . . . the terrible Dr. Pyre?" Magnus asked cautiously. He spoke the word *terrible* with strange emphasis—almost tenderness.

"Gone," said Theo softly. "Into the candlelight."

Magnus looked thoughtful. "Ah." He followed Theo out of the dungeon. "So you know."

There was a moment's silence. Theo frowned. "Magnus, did you know who Dr. Pyre was all along?" he gasped.

Magnus put a gnarled old finger to his lips. "The mysteries must be respected," he said. "For now, at least."

Snuffling keenly along the cracked and rubble-strewn passages, the smoglings soon uncovered more captives. As Theo peered through the bars in the gloom, he was greeted with an unexpected outburst of cheers. There, still locked in their cells, were Sam, Freddie, and all the other slaves.

"Theo!" Sam cried with delight. "Grandad! I knew you'd save us!"

"About time too," grumbled Freddie. And everyone cheered again.

CHAPTER 40

VIGILANT

A GRINNING ORPHEUS OFFICER, his face grimy, his uniform burnt and ragged, ran from the main door of the Furnace.

"Sir," he called to Captain Chloe Cripps. "I think we've got some good news for you!"

Chloe looked up eagerly. Frustrated in her attempts to break through the wall of flames, she had sent men down into the tunnels below the Furnace to hunt for any signs of life. Now, on the heels of the Orpheus guard, a soot-blackened mob of survivors emerged from the main door.

"Theo!"

Chloe ran towards her friends, who all seemed to

be coming out of the ruins at once. A jabbering crowd of smoglodytes sprang out of the doorway too, adding their gleeful howls to the celebration.

A bandaged, drained-looking Colonel Fairchild limped across the broken ground to give Theo a rather shaky salute. In a hopeful voice, he posed the question in all their minds.

"Mission accomplished?"

Before Theo could answer, Skun sprang into view and danced around him with a crazy grin on his face.

"We did it, didn't we?" Skun asked. "We smashed Dr. Pyre and his disgusting crelp? Tell me we won!"

Theo didn't know what to say. Magnus caught his eye.

The truth isn't always welcome, Theo thought. *There is a right time and a wrong time for it*. He knew that now. It wouldn't be right to reveal that Dr. Pyre had been the original Candle Man—that his desperate battle with the Philanthropist had led him to become dark, destructive, and bitter against all mankind.

"Dr. Pyre won't bother us anymore," said Theo finally.

"Yoo-woo-hooo!" cried the smoglings.

"You are the dreadest of the dread," said Skun with great respect.

"I never doubted him for a minute," said Freddie Dove, trying to beat the ash out of the remains of his frock coat.

Theo had been glancing around anxiously. "Did anyone see a—a garghoul?" he asked. "He was in the fortress too."

The thought of his horned ally made Theo feel uneasy. Lord Wickland had claimed that Tristus had tried to lead the garghouls in an uprising against mankind. Could it be true? There had always been a cloud over the garghoul, a mystery of some unhappy kind. Theo wasn't sure now if he wanted to face the creature or not.

"The proud one has flown," said Skun. "We held up the whole cavern together and saved all these horrible polices." He grimaced at Colonel Fairchild and his team. "Then the ungrateful melch flitted away."

"But he was blind—"

"Yes, I know," Skun interrupted. "But the stubborn golamphous said that the stone would talk to him and tell him the way. The way where, I don't know."

Theo smiled. So the garghoul was gone. But Theo's heart felt lighter, somehow. Tristus had played a part in saving everyone, then chosen to disappear. It was typical of the mysterious asra-ghoul.

Just then there was a stir among the Orpheus guards on the bridge. One of the officers posted at the entrance to the Well Chamber was crying out.

"They're here! They're here!"

Some kind of rescue force was arriving. Swarming down the tunnel from the Well Chamber were dozens of men and women in blue versions of the Orpheus uniform. Smart, clean, brisk, they were a sharp contrast with the disheveled mob that had survived the battle with the crelp.

"Excellent," said Colonel Fairchild, recovering a little of his composure. He even managed a fleeting smile. "Lord Gold said there would be a recovery force after the victory. They'll help the civilians back to the surface."

Sam nodded. "Best place for them."

"That includes you," Fairchild snapped at Sam.

"We're not civilians," Sam objected. "We're the Society of Unrelenting Vigilance!"

Freddie grinned at Sam's indignant red face. "The time for griping is over," he said. "Time to sit back and lap up the praise . . . the brave and glorious survivors! I expect I shall dine out on this adventure for years—and not on crelp moss and lime water!"

Theo said good-bye to Sam and Magnus, who were among the first to be allowed to return to the surface, and home. He longed to go with them, but Chloe had told him that one or two Orpheus duties still remained.

Watching his friends departing across the rock bridge to the Well Chamber, Theo felt a little finger dig him in the ribs.

"We're leaving," piped up Skun. "Too many humans!" He bowed to Theo. "I'm taking my tribe out of here," he said. "Good-bye, great Candle Hand. We shall always be brothers now."

Theo smiled. He liked that idea. "You won't change sides again?" Theo asked.

"Ah, well," said Skun. "It would be easy to promise that. But don't forget what great liars we smogs are."

Skun bowed towards Colonel Fairchild. "This victory was brought to you courtesy of the Society of Dread. Our dreadfulness is always at your disposal."

He sprang away, cackling. Theo watched as the smoglodytes disappeared like little shadows into the cracks in the ground. Finally, only humans remained, and suddenly the world seemed a little drabber for it.

Down Street Headquarters was silent. The corridors were lined with the returned Orpheus forces — those that had survived. The lucky unscathed ones supported the wounded.

Theo walked slowly through the ranks. Many heads turned to follow his progress as he passed, covered in ash, burnt crelp slime, scratches, and scars.

In the central hall, Lord Gold was waiting. There was a hush from the men as Theo walked up to their leader.

"I want to hear it from your own lips, Theo," Lord Gold said gravely. "Is Dr. Pyre gone? Did you see him destroyed, with your own eyes?"

Theo nodded. At first it seemed as if his voice would not come. Then he managed a quiet reply.

"He's gone, yes."

Lord Gold smiled. Suddenly the room erupted with cheers of relief and cries of emotion from those who had witnessed a day of terrible deeds. Some had tears streaking their faces.

"A great day, Theo," Lord Gold said. "We did it."

Theo nodded. "Yes, sir," he said. "We did."

Everywhere the Orpheus forces were talking—some slumped in chairs, others receiving medical attention. Everyone was reliving the events of the day. Through the hubbub, Theo was amazed to see a pristine figure in a white suit approaching. The figure acknowledged Theo with a tight little smile.

"Lord Dove!" Theo gasped.

The Ex-chief Benevolence of the Society of Good Works looked refreshed and resplendent. His son, Freddie, still caked in the grime of the furnaces, stood happily by his side.

"Well done, Master Wickland," Lord Dove said. "I knew the Candle Man would succeed. I showed great wisdom in sending you down there when I did. I've always been clever like that."

Freddie grinned. "Seems like Father has turned over a new leaf," he said cheerfully. "A day of wonders all around. There might be hope for the Dove family yet."

"But Lord Dove!" Theo gasped. "What are you doing here?"

Lord Gold appeared by Theo's side, beaming. His Lordship was the only person wearing the black Orpheus uniform who was not exhausted and filthy.

"A new age, Theo," he said. "With Dr. Pyre gone, and with me in charge of law and order in this city, it's a fresh start. The police pulled in Lord Dove a short while ago. I've decided that he, and everyone else in the Society of Good Works who was still on the run, shall receive a full pardon."

Theo was surprised, but he gave a tired smile. "That's . . . That's what I wanted too," he said a little uncertainly. "A new start. No more enemies."

"Exactly." Lord Gold smiled at everyone.

"With you in charge, Lord Commissioner," Lord Dove said, "it really will be a golden age!"

The room started to fill up with other dignitaries and police officials. Lord Gold received congratulations from them for the success of the mission. The Dodo had been right, Theo reflected. No one seemed to mention the role the Society of Dread had played at all.

Strangely, Theo rather liked it that way. He and Chloe took the first opportunity to make themselves scarce.

———

"So you didn't tell Lord Gold that Dr. Pyre was really Lord Wickland?" Magnus said to Theo that night, as they all gathered around the open fire in the tiny grate at the cemetery keeper's cottage. Sam passed around some hefty slices of homemade flapjack, burnt to a crisp around the edges.

"No," Theo replied, scooting over to make room for Chloe on the lumpy old red sofa. "I didn't want my ancestor to be remembered . . . only for the shadow he became."

"Well, I'm glad you told *us* the whole truth," Chloe said.

Sam looked slightly puzzled. "Why didn't you want to stay at the victory bash, Theo, and lap up the glory? You'll be the police's number one man now, London's great hero!" Sam gave a big grin, but no one else joined in.

"It seemed wrong," Theo sighed. "Everyone talking about a golden age, when for all we know, Lord Wickland was right—there might a bigger danger out there, a menace greater than any we've faced before."

"Ah, Theo," said Chloe, nursing a chipped mug of dark coffee. "That's very vigilant of you."

"Is it?" For the first time in hours, Theo felt a smile flicker on his face.

"That's what being the Candle Man is all about," she said. "Shining a light into the dark places where other people don't want to look. They want cheers, champagne, glory, and happily-ever-after—"

"While we," interrupted Sam, "are always looking

for new trouble, new menaces—and a hundred and one reasons to be miserable."

"Are there really a hundred and one?" Theo asked.

"Oh, yes," Chloe replied with a smile. "In fact, I've got them all written down. If you're very good, I'll let you see the whole list tomorrow."

"Great," Theo sighed, and bit bravely into one of Sam's cakes.

ACKNOWLEDGMENTS

The author would like to thank Regina Griffin, Nico Medina, Alison Weiss, and Mary Albi at Egmont USA, for their energy and insight in helping to unleash the Society of Dread upon the world. Great thanks also to Rachel Boden and Ali Dougal at Egmont UK, for all their dedication and hard work. Thanks, too, to Alice Barker, for wanting to know what happened next.

Stay vigilant for . . .

CANDLE MAN

BOOK THREE

THE WAY
OF THE DODO

Coming from Egmont USA
in Spring 2012

ABOUT THE AUTHOR

GLENN DAKIN continues to reveal the secrets of Theo and the legendary Candle Man, whom he introduced in the first book of the series, *The Society of Unrelenting Vigilance*. Dakin has written for many comics and children's TV shows, including the BBC's *Shaun the Sheep*, for which he won an International Emmy Award. He lives in Cambridge, England, with his family. You can visit him online at www.glenndakin.com.

The art for the jacket of this book was created by Greg Swearingen using acrylic paint, ink, watercolor, and colored pencil on paper. The interior frontispiece was created using graphite on paper.

––•⊁•––

The text was set in thirteen on seventeen-point Cochin, a font named for Charles-Nicolas Cochin le Jeune, an eighteenth-century engraver to the French court, and designed in the early twentieth century by Georges Peignot.

––•⊁•––

The book was typeset by Arlene Goldberg. The book was printed and bound at Berryville Graphics in Berryville, Virginia. The Production Manager was Danielle Monaco, and the Managing Editor was Nico Medina.